Abby Donavan came to the small beach community of Crystal Cove to start over. After a painful affair broke her heart and derailed her burgeoning career, taking over management for the just-opened bed-and-breakfast was the safe choice. In this sleepy town, Abby figured she could bury her memories and forget the pain.

When the chance to have her own hotel falls into her lap, though, she can't resist the temptation. Making the old Riverside Inn into the showplace she's always dreamed of running offers the second chance she never expected.

Abby didn't expect another kind of second chance to land on her doorstep at the same time. Ryland Kent wants to help her bring the Riverside back to life, and his passion for restoration is irresistible. But as much as she wants to ignore it, she can't help seeing another spark in his eyes . . . one that offers to reignite her own flame.

Sometimes the path to a happily-ever-after is anything but smooth.

THE PATH

TAWDRA KANDLE

The Path
Copyright © 2015 Tawdra Kandle

Cover by Once Upon a Time Covers
Formatting by Champagne Formats

ISBN-978-1-68230-267-5

dedication

To all my girlfriends, from childhood through homeschooling to authordom: you each hold a special piece of my heart, and I can't imagine life without you all as part of it. Even when we're far apart, or when we don't see each other for long periods of time . . . know I've got your back, just as I know you've got mine.

prologue

"NO, NO, NO!" I SHOOK my head and pressed my lips together, trying to tamp down my frustration level as I stood outside the bright yellow house. "You've got the flag facing the wrong direction. It's got to come off the pole and go back on the other way."

The men standing on the edge of the roof on the second story of the Hawthorne House Bed and Breakfast exchanged glances that I couldn't quite read, but I was pretty sure they weren't ones of admiration for me.

"Hey, Ms. D., don't you think it's okay if they stay like this? No one's going to notice whether the leaves face this way or that." Lester Black put his hands on his hips and stared me down. It wasn't the first time we'd had this kind of battle, but thank Christ, it was likely to be one of the last. Today's changeover from our summer décor to the autumn flags and flowers was my last official duty as manager of this bed and breakfast on the main street of Crystal Cove.

"No, actually, Lester, I don't think it's okay. When have I thought it was okay to take short cuts or do things the wrong way just because they were easier? Now are you two going to fix those flags, or am I going to come up there and do it myself?" I planted my hands on my hips and leveled my most lethal bitch stare at the men.

"Oh, for crying out loud, Les, just do it." The other man, a little shorter and stockier than his co-worker, shook his head. "You know Logan'll have a shit fit if he finds out we let her climb up here. And she will." He cast me a baleful glare, and I only barely managed to not stick out my tongue in return.

Be chill, Ab. You're the boss. You're in charge. Don't give an inch. Stand firm, and they'll do what you say.

I could almost hear my father's words in my head, and I smiled a little. Colin Donavan never had to raise his voice to get things done. He just spoke slowly and precisely, with that underlying core of steel, and everyone jumped to do his bidding.

His daughter, on the other hand, had to make use of the bitch stare with alarming regularity just to get two workmen to fix flags or set up flowerpots. Yeah, no matter how much of my dad's hotel-running acumen I'd inherited, I still didn't seem to be able to command the same respect he did. Maybe I never would.

"Abigail Donavan, the fairest of them all." A familiar voice approached from behind me, and I grinned just before two arms wrapped around my shoulders. "Every time I see

2

you, you're more gorgeous. What's your secret?"

I leaned my head back against Alex Nelson's broad chest. "Must be clean living."

He sighed heavily. "Well, then, I'm fucked."

I laughed, and he joined me, keeping one arm around me as he stood at my side, looking up at the house. "She really is a beauty, isn't she?"

"She really is." I swallowed hard. I wasn't really leaving the Hawthorne House far behind me. My new job was just up the road, and I'd be able to come down here any time I wanted to make sure everything was running smoothly. But we'd been each other's first, this house and me. I was her first manager, and she was my first B&B, my first solo managing job. Working here, in this quaint little Florida beach town, for Jude Hawthorne and Logan Holt, had been my salvation after the unholy mess I'd made up in Boston. She was always going to hold a special place in my heart.

"Transitions are hard." Alex wasn't looking down at me anymore, but his fingers tightened around my arm. "And scary. But you know you're leaving her in good hands, right?"

"The best." I stood on tiptoe to kiss his cheek, rough with the little bit of scruff I'd noticed he always left on his jaw. "You and Cal are going to rock this job. I couldn't have left her with anyone else."

"And you're not really leaving. You'll be so close at the Riverside, we'll practically be able to hear the hammers from down here. We can walk to meet up halfway for lunch every day, and I'll give you an update on all things Hawthorne."

"Don't be silly. You don't work for me, and you don't

owe me any updates. Jude and Logan'll keep you accountable." I smirked. "Besides, I'll know what's going on when I make my midnight walks down here, peeking in at the windows and skulking in the garden."

"Well, that's . . . creepy." Alex grimaced. "I just made a note to myself to add privacy shutters to the list of things I need to get for our apartment."

"As if that would stop me." I paused, watching as Lester and his cohort replaced the flag poles, with the autumn leaves facing the correct way this time. "Nice job, boys."

Lester waved, but I wasn't entirely certain all of his fingers were participating equally in the action.

"Did he just give you the finger?" Alex squinted up.

I shrugged. "I'm choosing not to notice. One thing I've learned is that sometimes we have to choose our battles and be happy about the ones we win." I slid Alex's hand into mine. "Come on inside, and I'll fix you a drink to celebrate my last day as manager of the Daniel Hawthorne Bed and Breakfast."

"And the first day of the rest of your life." Alex squeezed my fingers. "I'll drink to that."

chapter one

Ryland

SHE WAS GORGEOUS.

And I was in love.

I could always tell right away. Love at first sight was something I believed in, just like I believed in the magic of Christmas, the existence of angels and the hope of a World Series win for the Philadelphia Phillies.

Well, two out of three ain't bad.

It usually happened for me within the first few minutes. I didn't have to hear a word; I could just take her in, watch her and feel the hum of possibilities. I loved that giddy sense of hope that filled me during the early days, when everything was potential and dreams, before reality came crashing in and we had to deal with problems and snafus. Before my

5

eyes were forced to see that beneath the beauty lay broken-ness and decay.

But for now, all I could see was the future, like a vision spread out before me. She was both the vision and the future. Yeah, there was no doubt in my mind.

The Riverside Inn was a dream come true.

"So you gonna stand there and drool all day, or you gonna get to work?" Lincoln punched me in the shoulder, grinning.

"Yeah, I might. Drool, I mean." I slid my gaze to his. "She's pretty damn drool-worthy."

"Oh, hell, Ry. No way. This one?" Linc glanced at the sprawling building, disbelief in his eyes. "Aw, dammit. You got the look. I see it on your face. You got the look, and that means you're attached already."

I laughed. "Pretty sad that you know me that well. Yeah, she's a go. I signed the papers day before yesterday."

"Shit, man." Linc shook his head. "This one is . . . it's bad, buddy. I saw the reports. Most of the main building's structurally unsound. Tearing her down to the stud's a given, but we may have to go father than that."

"I know." I'd read the same reports. The old hotel had been empty for years, sitting on this huge chunk of land on the outskirts of Crystal Cove, Florida. One owner and then another had made plans, only to abandon them. That was okay, because I knew she'd been waiting for me all along.

"You know, yet you sign the contract. You commit to this building. To this project. And you don't only commit yourself, you commit me and the rest of the company, too. Did you think to ask me what I thought before you put your

John Hancock down on those papers? Why'd you bother asking me to come up here if you'd already made up your mind?"

I shrugged. "Linc, I gave you a chance at partnership three years ago, and then again early this year. You turned me down both times. I value your opinion, and I try to listen, but if you want a real say in the projects we choose, then you've got to be a partner. Because right now, I'm where the buck stops. So you have to trust that if I said yes, I know how we can make it work. And I wanted you to see her because I know this project will start percolating in the back of your mind now. You'll call me at midnight in a few days with ideas." I elbowed my friend in the ribs. "Besides, have we ever failed yet?"

"Came damn close in San Francisco." Linc muttered the words darkly, and I tried not to wince.

"Yeah, but it all worked out in the end." The old house we'd agreed to turn into a bar and restaurant for a couple in California had seemed like an easy job when I took it. We'd been a solid two weeks into the rehab when one of the guys discovered extensive structural damage, probably from one of the earthquakes. It was too late to turn around, too late to back out, and I was damned glad I had enough capital saved to cover the extra manpower and work hours, not to mention the supplies. We'd eeked it out, barely breaking even . . . but we did it. And now that trendy little bar was getting rave reviews from all the fancy-schmancy food critics on the West Coast.

"Barely." Linc shook his head. "Well, nothing we can do about this now. You committed us, so we're all in, for better or for worse. I'm heading back down to Vero, finish up the details and the punch out on the salon. Then if it's cool with you, I thought I might swing over to Mont Devlin for a little while."

I kept my face expressionless as I nodded. "Sure. Of course it is. Gonna check in, see the kids a little?"

"Yeah, thought I might." His mouth pinched together, and I could see his jaw tighten under the thin layer of his beard. "For whatever time they'll give me, anyway."

There wasn't anything I could say to him. Nothing could change the past or make this situation any less painful. So I didn't insult him with stupid meaningless words. Instead, I gave him a light punch to the shoulder. Linc understood; his lips twisted into what passed for a grim smile, and he shrugged.

"You take what you need, you know that." I leveled my gaze at him, making sure he understood me. "When you're ready, come on back here. I'll put you to work."

"Sounds like a plan." He took one step away, toward where I assumed his truck was waiting, before pausing to glance at me over his shoulder. "You got a place to crash here yet, or you still got to find something?"

"I have a place in town. The owners have a friend— Cooper Davis, he's actually a carpenter, a woodworker. He's going to do the decorative wood and the built-ins here on the Riverside. Anyway, I guess he just moved in with his girlfriend, and he's got an apartment he doesn't need at the moment. It's furnished, close to the site and best of all, free. Cooper says he's just happy to have me there to keep my eye on his shop at night."

"Sweet." Linc had regained a little of his calm. "I'll get in touch when I'm back. Where're you setting up the guys?"

"Motel the next town over. It's got restaurants, stores, bars . . . all the stuff they need to be happy while they're here." I considered briefly and shook my head. "And probably enough for them to get into trouble, unfortunately. But we'll deal with that when it comes."

"Sure. Although I've got a feeling this one's going to keep them so busy, they may be too tired to cause problems after work."

I grinned. "You could be right."

Linc laughed and started walking again. "I'll be in touch. Don't have too much fun before I get here."

"Fun doesn't start 'til you do, buddy." I yelled at his departing back, trying to ignore the slump in his shoulders. I'd known Lincoln for over ten years. We'd met on one of my earliest jobs, when I'd just started out. I'd been an unhappy combination of cocky and homesick, carrying a giant chip on my shoulder to hide my terror that I might fail. He was a few years older than me, already married with a kid, and he'd taken me under his wing. When I'd launched my own company finally, offering Linc a partnership had been a given. But his life had changed radically by then, and he wasn't ready for the added responsibility. Or so he claimed.

Still, we all knew Linc was as much a part of this company's leadership as I was. He might not've had the title, but he put in the time and did the work. I just wished that it gave him some peace of mind, something that had been missing from my friend for far too long.

The sun was sinking lower in the sky, and I rubbed my

jaw, thinking. I was tempted to go in and check out a few sections of the old hotel that I hadn't gotten a chance to really explore during my short walk-through with Logan Holt a few days back. We had a rule at this stage in the game: nobody, no matter how experienced or careful, was supposed to be in the building alone. In these rehab projects, we couldn't always predict when a supporting wall might decide to give way, or when a cracked foundation might shift. The guidelines I'd laid down myself stated that one person needed to be outside while at least two went in together. Breaking that rule was grounds for instant firing.

But hell, I was the boss. I knew my way around these old beauties, and I had an uncanny sense of where I might not be safe. Stepping inside a little ways wasn't going to hurt anyway. I checked my cell and made sure I had both battery life and signal before ducking beneath the yellow caution tape.

The Riverside had been built over a hundred years ago, before Crystal Cove had even really existed. She'd been designed to cater to the river traffic; although the Cove was known for its beaches, they weren't as popular a century before as they were now. Instead, the hotel had welcomed guests who were meandering down the waterways from Jacksonville to the interior of the state, which had still been largely wilderness in some places.

I imagined what she must've been like then; pretty and graceful, her two main wings sprawling over a large expanse of green lawn that went to the edge of the river. Wide verandas beckoned weary travelers, and the huge kitchens produced some of the best food south of Savannah. I could picture it, and I wanted it for her again. I knew I could make it happen.

Stepping carefully along the shadowed corridor, I paused, squatting to examine some partially-rotted molding. I pulled a small folding knife out of my pocket and carefully pried off a piece. I rubbed my thumb over the front and smiled. *Oh, yeah.* I could work with this. Wasn't easy to find this kind of decorative trim anymore, but I'd taken a peek into Cooper Davis's shop, and I was pretty damn sure he could replicate it. Might take some sweet talking, but he seemed like a good guy, and he was undoubtedly passionate about his work. Well, so was I, about mine. I'd make this happen.

Standing again, I moved into a large open space which I decided must've been either a dining room or some kind of reception hall. The windows here went nearly to the floor. It would've been something to see in its time, I mused, even though now not one pane of glass remained. There wasn't even a decent frame left. That was okay. We'd bring them back.

A cool breeze blew through the room, and despite the stifling heat in the hotel, I felt goose flesh raise on my arms. I glanced out the gaping holes that had once been French doors leading to the side porch. For a moment, just a split second, I could've sworn I'd seen a movement, something more than just the swaying of the trees. But although I stood frozen for a while, I didn't see anything again.

"Ghosties." I muttered the word to myself, shaking my head. All of us who worked this job, who spent hours and days and weeks and months inside ancient buildings that wanted to come back to life, were familiar with the feeling that we weren't always alone. It didn't surprise me anymore; after all this time, I was now convinced that certain experiences, both traumatic and ecstatic, left an imprint on the walls of the building where they happened. I'd never seen a ghost or even suspected one might be haunting a house I was working on, but it didn't mean I didn't believe. It didn't mean I thought they didn't exist.

And right now, in this place, I had the distinct sense of being . . . observed. As though someone were keeping an eye on me, not yet sure whether I was here for harm or for help. I stuck my hands in the front pockets of my jeans and spoke out loud, not shouting but not whispering, either.

"Hey, there. Just in case you're wondering, I'm here to make this place live again. My crew and I want to restore the hotel, make it just as beautiful as it once was. And as long as you're on our side, not messing with our stuff or our work, you're welcome to stay. We won't bother you."

My voice echoed in the empty hallway, but once the last word had died away, I could've sworn I heard something like . . . a sigh. Like the patient breath of someone who'd heard it all before. Well, this time I was going to make sure it really happened.

"We're going to make her shine again, just you wait and see." I turned and stalked deeper into the hotel, suddenly more eager to get in and out than I'd been a few minutes before.

On the other side of the airy lobby, a corridor lined with guest rooms stretched around. I paused for a moment to snap a picture with my camera phone of the remnants of the staircase that opened behind the reception desk. It looked like it might be marble underneath the old rug. If it had had a bannister at some point, the wood was long gone. I wondered if Cooper could handle that kind of project.

Just as I stepped out of the hallway into one of the first rooms on the right, I heard a noise. My body tensed, going alert; besides the obvious structural dangers, another reason we didn't let anyone venture into an empty building project alone was that often, depending on the location, we might run across a squatter or even a group of homeless people. The last thing I needed was to surprise someone who might act—and act violently—if surprised.

I leaned against the inside wall of the room I'd just entered, waiting and listening. And a few minutes later, I heard it again—the sound of a step, a footfall. It wasn't loud, which made me think I might be safe from a vagrant; in my experience, they didn't tend to sneak around. A moment later, there was a soft noise, as though someone had brushed up against a wall. I froze, and the hair on the back of my neck stood on end. That same sense of someone or something watching clutched me.

I gritted my teeth. *What the hell was wrong with me?* I wasn't afraid of being alone in a falling-down building, and I damned sure wasn't scared of a noise that might or might not be a spook. Muttering a curse under my breath and trying to ignore the unease I felt, I stepped back out into the hall, ready to laugh at myself for being a wuss.

The scream hit me first. It was Jamie Lee Curtis-worthy, and I swore the exposed studs in this part of the hotel shook with the vibration. The sound almost stopped my heart, giving my brain less time to register the figure standing in front of me.

It was a woman. That fact filtered through first. And she looked pretty damn solid, so chances were good she wasn't a ghost. She was shorter than me by four or five inches, I guessed. Her jeans and T-shirt were more evidence that she was likely a trespasser instead of a lost spirit; anyone haunting this old place was likely to wear clothes from fifty years ago or more, since the hotel had been empty so long.

The ghost-who-wasn't-a-ghost had long hair that was dark, nearly black, setting off skin so pale that it almost glowed. She had the silky strands in a high pony tail, though a few pieces had gotten loose and curled around her face. Her green eyes were startling in their intensity, especially because at the moment, they were wide with shock and fear.

"Jesus, Mary and Joseph!" The words came bursting out of my mouth as soon as I had enough breath to speak again. "What the hell are you doing skulking around here? Didn't you notice the, oh, fifty or so NO TRESPASSING signs?"

"Me?" The chick planted both hands on her hips and glared up at me. "I'm not trespassing, buddy. I'm supposed to be here. This is *my* project. What the hell are *you* doing here?"

I thrust my hands into my back pockets and rocked on my heels. This girl was something else. The eyes that had been terrified a few minutes ago now snapped with a strong mad. Her tongue darted out and licked the full lips, and I'd have been lying if I'd said that didn't distract me just a little.

But I managed to bring my attention back around. "Nice try, sweetheart. Now listen, you just get out of here and don't come back again, and I won't call the cops. I don't know what you think you're doing, but—"

"*You* won't call the cops? Oh, that's rich. Tell you what, you go ahead and call the police. They know me. They'll tell you I have every right to be here. Or call Logan Holt." She stopped talking, and her brows knit together. "Why am I even trying to justify myself to you? You're the one who's in the wrong here. How about you hit the road?"

She had balls, I had to give her that. Or whatever the female equivalent of balls was. I thought about that for a second and then shook my head. I was getting off track again. But one thing she'd said did make me wonder. She'd mentioned Logan and said this hotel was her project. She seemed so certain, I was starting to question my own sanity.

"How do you know Logan?" That seemed like a reasonable place to start.

Her eyes narrowed. "I know Logan because I've been working for him and for his wife, Jude, for the last three years. How do you know him?"

Okay, this was getting weirder. "He hired me to do the restoration on this hotel. I just signed the papers on Wednesday."

Understanding dawned on her face. "You're the contractor?"

I didn't roll my eyes, but I wanted to. God, did I want to. "I'm the restoration specialist."

One of her eyebrows arched, and the corner of her lip curled. "Oh, pardon me. Restoration specialist." She all but made the air quotes, and I wanted to hit something. Not her, of course—I wasn't a dick—but something.

"Yeah. That's right. And just who are you, if you don't mind?"

She straightened, as though she was trying to make herself look taller. "I'm Abigail Donavan."

"Okay, and . . .?" I rolled my hand in a keep-going gesture.

"This is my hotel."

It was my turn to quirk an eyebrow. "I was under the impression this place belongs to Logan and Jude Holt. At least their names were on the papers I signed."

She nodded. "Logan and Jude own the hotel. But they hired me to run it. They gave me carte blanche to make it work. So for all intents and purposes, it's mine."

"Oh, yeah?" I was ready with a smartass response, but something niggled at my memory. I had a vague recollection of Logan mentioning someone who'd be dealing with me during the rehab. I couldn't remember if he'd referred to her by name, but unless this lady was bat-shit crazy, it was probably her. *Shit.*

I knew, logically, that I needed to make nice with her if she was going to be calling the shots. Restoring a property like this was a delicate balance of delivering the client's vision without compromising my own artistic ideals and historical values. Getting off on the wrong foot wouldn't be a good idea.

But no one told my mouth that, apparently, since it started yammering of its own accord. "If you're so important with your *carte blanche* and all, why weren't you at the meetings I had this week with Logan and Jude?"

A delicate pink stained her cheeks. "I had a few days of

vacation, and I had to go out of town. Otherwise, of course I would've been there." She swallowed, and I knew that I'd hit a sensitive spot, even though I had no clue what it was. "Trust me when I say that Jude and Logan didn't have a problem with me missing the meetings. They know me. They know I'm fully capable of running this place and making it into a showpiece. Like I said, I've been working for them for three years, and I've never let them down." There was considerable pride in her tone.

"What exactly did you do for them before this?" I knew that Logan and Jude owned several different businesses; he was an architect, and Jude ran a beach-front restaurant that had been in her family for generations, but they'd also invested in some local properties. From what I'd gathered, Logan had been in business with Jude's late husband, a contractor who'd been the Hawthorne in Holt/Hawthorne Enterprises.

"I managed the Hawthorne House. It's the bed and breakfast in the middle of town." She paused, gauging whether or not I knew what she was referring to. "Jude and Logan own it."

"I know what you're talking about." Jude had explained that they'd never owned a hotel, but that their B&B was very successful. I guessed that meant this Donavan chick was good at what she did. *Damn.* "So you're going to manage both of them now? Seems like a crazy idea."

She thrust out her bottom lip. "I could do it. Believe me, if I wanted, I could—" She snapped her mouth shut, as though she'd been about to reveal a deep, dark secret to me. "But anyway, I'm not. Jude and Logan hired a couple to take over the Hawthorne House, so I can focus all my energy here." She smiled, but it was too brittle to be real and didn't quite reach her eyes. "So lucky you. You get me all to yourself for the duration of this—what did you call it? Restoration. I'll be here every day, checking out the work. I'll expect to be consulted on all decisions." She crossed her arms over her chest, bringing my eyes to her cleavage.

I'm a guy. I couldn't help checking out her rack. It wasn't big by any means; the black cotton that stretched over her boobs outlined what looked like a decent palm full. Of course, a dude would have to wear body armor to get close enough to touch her tits, as prickly as she was. I couldn't imagine it, and I had a damned good imagination.

I lifted my eyes and realized by the expression of outraged disbelief on her face that I'd been caught eyeing up her boobs. *Great.* I needed damage control, and I needed it fast.

"I'm sure that won't be a problem." *That's right, Ry, suck up. Schmooze her a little, get on her good side, and the rest of this job'll be a breeze.* "I've never had a problem working with any client."

She smiled again, and while it seemed to be a little more genuine, her gaze held a chill. I couldn't help thinking she reminded me of the Ice Queen from an old story my mom had read to me growing up.

"But then you've never worked with me, have you . . . what did you say your name was?" She frowned. Not knowing my name had thrown her off-balance a little, and I realized I'd just discovered something important about Ms. Abigail Donavan: she didn't like to be unprepared or in the dark about her work. Not getting my name upfront had been a mistake, and she'd just revealed it.

I could afford to be a little magnanimous, all things considered. "Ryland Kent." I stuck out my hand. "Restoration specialist."

She stared at my outstretched fingers for the space of two breaths before uncrossing her arms and shaking my hand. "Good to meet you, Mr. Kent. I'm sure we'll get along fine, assuming you remember who's in charge."

I gave her hand a little extra grip, just to make my point. "Believe me, that's one thing I never forget, *Ms.* Donavan."

Our eyes locked, and neither of us loosened our hands. I wasn't going to back down. While I always wanted to make the client happy, it was essential to establish my own position up front, and no way was I letting this stubborn woman best me. No fucking way.

We might've stood like that forever, neither of us willing to give up gracefully, but there was a loud and sudden noise from within the room behind me. We both jumped and dropped hands. Abigail wrapped her arms around her middle.

"What was that?" She was whispering, as though afraid someone might be close by and overhear us.

I shrugged. "Could be anything." I took a step backward and scanned the empty room. It looked exactly as it had when I'd been in it a little bit ago, except . . . I frowned. In the middle of the room lay a wrench. It wasn't mine; it was an ancient tool, rusted and worn, looking like it'd been left here by some repairman decades before. That in itself wasn't unusual, of course, but I knew it hadn't been there earlier.

"What is it?" Abigail stood close behind me, so that I could feel the heat of her body on my back.

"I don't see anything. Except that wrench wasn't there before. I was looking at this room when I heard you coming, and I know it was empty."

She bit the side of her lip. "Maybe you just didn't notice it."

"I would've seen it. I was checking out the floor, and that wrench is right in the middle of the damn floor. Would've been hard to miss it."

"Maybe it fell from somewhere. You know, you were messing with stuff. Maybe something came loose and it just fell."

"Oh, yeah, because wrenches fall out of thin air all the time. There's no place in that room it could've fallen from. Use your eyes."

She was annoyed, I could tell, but this time I realized that it was because she was feeling the same creeped-out jitters I was. I decided to give her an out.

"Look, it could've been anything. You're right, maybe I just didn't see it before. But we should probably both get out of here now anyway. We have a company rule about not being in an unsafe structure alone. I don't think this place is in danger of falling on our heads, but you never know." I thought about San Francisco and repressed a shudder.

Abigail didn't argue with me, which I decided only proved how shaken up she was. We followed the silent corridors around to where I'd come in, at the old service entrance in the back. Once we were clear of the hotel, I noticed that she hesitated, glancing back and up at the windows, unease written all over her face.

I started to walk back up toward the street side of the

property, where I'd left my truck, but she didn't follow.

"I'm parked by the river." She pointed in the opposite direction.

I bit back a sigh of impatience. It was getting dark, and while I didn't think there was anything dangerous between here and Abigail's car, my mom had taught me that a gentleman always saw a lady to safety. I turned and stalked past her, toward the river.

"I didn't mean you have to baby-sit me to my car." She was walking fast to catch up to me. "I was just being polite, telling you why I was going this way."

"Yeah, well, it's getting dark, and old buildings like this tend to attract vagrants. Mostly they're harmless, but I'd rather not put that theory to the test."

She was silent until we reached the old gravel and crushed-shell lot where one dark sedan was parked. Figured she'd drive something like that. It looked like her: cool and reserved. A little stand-offish. But just maybe it was hotter under the hood than anyone might think.

I gave my head a little shake. *Where did that come from?* I wasn't interested in what was or wasn't under Abigail Donavan's hood, literal or otherwise.

"Why were you in the hotel?" The question jolted my attention back to her.

"I thought we'd established that. Because I'm going to work on it. Restore it."

She waved her hand. "Yes, yes, I know that. I meant, if there's a rule against being there alone, why were you?"

I shook my head. "I wanted to take another look without anyone to distract me. There were a few things I'd noticed but hadn't had time to check on more closely."

"But it's against the rules." The certainty in her voice told me more about the woman who stood in front of me. She was a rule-follower. A good girl. Not someone I should be messing with, and definitely not my type.

But on the other hand, good girls could be lots of fun, once I brought them around to my way of thinking.

I grinned and stepped closer to her, just enough that I was in her space. I could tell she wanted to move back, but she didn't. She stood her ground, daring me to try something. Anything.

I reached down as though I was going to touch her cheek, but at the last minute, I circled my hand around to grab her pony tail, giving it a sharp tug.

"Honey, don't you know rules are made to be broken?" I winked and stepped back, heading up the lawn toward my truck. "See you around, *Ms. Donavan*."

If I thought I'd gotten the last word and left her speechless, though, I was mistaken. Her voice floated through the still air.

"Oh, you can count on that, *Mr. Kent*."

I chuckled. *Oh, this was going to be fun.*

chapter two

Abby

" . . . and then he said, 'If you're so important, with your *carte blanche* and all, why weren't you at the meetings I had last week with Jude and Logan?" I drained my wine glass and set it down on the bar with a little more force than was necessary.

On the other side of that bar, my friend Emmy raised her eyebrows. "Whoa, there, Ab. Simmer down. You break Jude's wine glasses and you might lose your, uh, *carte blanche*."

I snorted. "Let me tell you, this guy's just lucky I didn't have anything handy to throw at him. I'm Irish, you know. We tend to get violent when we lose our tempers."

Emmy laughed. "Abby, you're probably one of the most

even-tempered people I know. I don't think I've ever seen you break a sweat or raise your voice, even when you were arguing with the handyman at the Hawthorne." She folded the bar towel and draped it over a hook behind the bar. "Ryland must've really hit a nerve to get you so worked up."

"Oh, you have no idea, Emmy. You don't know the man, but he's condescending and frustrating and rude."

"Actually, I've met him. I was dropping off pies last week when he was here to talk with Jude and Logan." She leaned a hip against the counter that ran the length of the kitchen. "He seemed okay to me."

"Hmph." I used one finger to inch the wine glass a little bit away from me. "Can you pour me some more, please? Just add it to my tab."

Emmy retrieved my favorite Pinot Grigio from the wine rack and uncorked it. "Sure you want a second glass? You've got a long walk home, don't forget." She winked at me.

Even as mad as I still was, I couldn't help a smirk. "Yeah, good point. I mean, getting across the restaurant would be tough enough, but navigating the fourteen steps up to the apartment? That's a killer. Maybe I should stop at one."

"Oh, live a little. If you're too sloshed to make it upstairs, I'll enlist some hot guy to toss you over his shoulder and carry you up."

I held the refilled glass between my fingers, taking a sip. "That's just what I need. A guy to complicate my life."

"Oh, I don't know. Maybe you do. You know, just a one-night thing. A hook-up, like the kids say." She grinned at me. "That's what I did, and I'm telling you, it was life-changing."

"Of course it was, because you hooked up with Cooper,

and it ended up being more than one night, didn't it?"

Emmy's face took on a rosy glow, and her smile shifted to dreamy. "Yeah, good point. But still, I highly recommend it." She leaned her elbows on the bar and dropped her voice. "Best sex of my life. Up to that point, of course. Since then, it's only gotten better."

I groaned. "Oh, would you shut up about the sex? It's not nice to brag about the gourmet meals you're eating when you're talking to a woman who's on the verge of starvation."

"That's a choice, Ab. You don't have to be starving. All you'd have to do is crook your finger and you'd have guys running."

"Away from me?"

Emmy rolled her eyes. "Smartass. Maybe swarming is the better word. Yeah, you'd have the guys swarming around you, like the drones around the queen bee."

I considered for a minute. "You know, that's a surprisingly accurate metaphor, since drones are the bees whose job is to mate with the queen. Well done."

"Izzy just finished a science project on the behavior of bees." Emmy shrugged. "Fascinating stuff. Cooper helped with it, too, and now the two of them are trying to talk me into keeping bees."

"Just what you need." I took another taste of my wine. "How's it going, by the way? Cooper living with you, I mean."

"So far, so good." She folded her arms over her chest. "I mean, it's only been a month. But I keep waiting for the other shoe to fall, you know? For my kids to annoy Cooper, or him to yell at them, or something like that. But they seem to be okay. Lex came down last weekend and stayed with us, and I thought that might be awkward, but it wasn't. It was actually fun to have everyone together. They all made breakfast for me on Saturday morning, and Izzy thinks she finally has a big sister."

"I'm so glad for you, Em." My eyes got a little misty. If anyone deserved a happy ending, it was my friend. She'd gotten married young and had three kids before her loser husband ran off to find better surfing. A lesser woman might've fallen apart, but Emmy Carter was not that woman. She'd opened her own pie business, taken on the job of weekend night manager here at the Riptide and managed to keep her family afloat. She and Cooper had been friends for a while before they'd finally given into a one-night fling that had turned into love.

"I'm glad for me, too." She picked up a plate of nachos that the cook had slid through the kitchen pass-between. I watched as she delivered them to a couple down the bar, laughed at something they said to her and returned to me. "And maybe it's because I'm happy and in love and all that disgusting shit, but I want to see you find someone, too."

"Good luck." I centered the bottom of my wine glass in the dead middle of the small white cocktail napkin beneath it and turned it in slow circles. "I'm pretty sure I'm destined for spinsterhood, Em."

"Bull. You're young, you're gorgeous, and you're smart. Guys are always checking you out."

I almost choked on my wine. "Oh, sure they are. I appreciate the sentiment, Emmy, but I know the score. I'm not exactly swimming in offers."

My friend's eyes clouded. "If that's true, it's only because you don't want them. And when a woman's closed-off like that, it shows. It's sort of a hands-off vibe. I've seen you when we go out, and it's as if a wall goes up. You're not the same fun girl I hang out with at the Hawthorne or at my house."

A weight settled in my chest. "I know. And honestly, I haven't been looking for a relationship or even just a hook-up. My work has to come first right now. It's the one thing I can depend on. I nearly forgot that once, and I'm not going to let it happen again."

Emmy refilled a bowl of nuts and slid it across to me. "Abby, you know I don't pry. I get that some things are private, and I've never pushed you to tell me all your secrets. But I'm here if you ever want to talk about anything." She worried her bottom lip between her teeth, as though she wasn't sure what to say next. "This is going to sound corny, but you really are my best friend. I didn't have many girlfriends growing up. When I was a kid, sure, but once we hit high school and I started dating Eddy, I didn't have time for anyone but him. Then I was married and had the kids, and . . . well, you know what came next. But now I have you and Jude. I love Jude, don't get me wrong, but I feel like you and I connected when we met. I tell you everything—"

"Hmph." I couldn't help interrupting her there. "Funny, I don't remember the long talks we had about you and Cooper when you first started to see each other last spring."

Emmy had the good grace to look sheepish. "You're right. I wanted to tell you, but then I thought Jude was trying to fix you up with him, and I didn't want it to get weird between us. And I didn't know what was happening, either. I thought it was just a one-time thing."

"You still could've told me." It had stung, I had to admit. I hadn't thought it would. But when Jude had confided in me months before that she'd seen Cooper's car at Emmy's house in the early-morning hours on a Saturday and shared her suspicions about the two of them, my first thought had been laced with hurt. Emmy and I had often commiserated about our singleness and lack-of-sex life, so the idea that she was getting some while still playing the woe-is-me card made me feel a little betrayed.

"I know, and I should have. I'm sorry. My only excuse is that I'm still new at the friend deal. I didn't tell anyone, not even my mom."

"I wouldn't think you would. I mean, I know you're pretty close to your mom, and she's totally cool, but I still wouldn't call her and share about the hot sex I was having." I shuddered at the thought. There were lines, and then there were *lines*.

"True. My mom and dad adore Cooper, and they're happy for me, but I think they're still having trouble adjusting to the idea that he's living with their little girl. Mom's been dropping some not-so-subtle hints about us getting married."

"Do you think you will?" I knew Cooper was gun-shy about marriage, having been twice divorced.

Emmy shrugged. "I don't know. Maybe. We've talked about it a little, but nothing definite. Izzy keeps asking me, but I think it's a combination of wanting to be a bridesmaid and maybe . . ." One side of her mouth twisted into a sort-of smile. "Maybe feeling like marriage would make this permanent. Sometimes I forget that Eddy skipping out affected them, too. He wasn't that great a dad, but he was still there. Mostly. And then he wasn't. I think my kids want to make sure Cooper's not going to do the same."

"He wouldn't. He's stupid in love with you, and he adores your kids, too. When I see you all together, I'm never sure if I want to cry or puke a little, it's so sweet."

"Aw, Ab, stop it with the gooey talk. You're going to make me cry." Emmy laughed. "Okay, kiddo, looks like Gritt's about ready to kick off the night. You want anything else before it gets loud and crazy in here?"

I shook my head. "Thanks, but no. I'm going to drag myself upstairs, take a long bath and go to bed."

"Does the noise down here bother you?" Emmy's forehead wrinkled.

"If I say yes, are you going to make them all be quiet?" I slid off the barstool. "Nah. I'll just put in my earbuds and crank up some of my own music. And once I fall asleep, I'm dead to the world."

"Must be strange, living up there after the cute little apartment you had at the B&B."

I lifted one shoulder. "I'm used to moving every other year or so. It's the life of a hotelier. Plus, this is temporary. Once we get the Riverside back in shape and all beautiful, I'll have my own personal suite right on site. I can't wait." Thinking of that brought back my earlier encounter with the contractor. Oh, wait—the *restoration specialist*. "That is, if I don't end up killing that renovations guy and going to prison."

The DJ chose that moment to open up his mic.

"Gooooooood evening, Crystal Cove! Welcome to Friday night at the Tiiiiiiiide!"

The crowd on the dance floor had swelled while I was sulking at the bar. They roared their approval at Gritt's welcome as he cranked up the volume on an oldie-but-goody— Bobby Rydell, singing about *Wildwood Days*. I smiled; although I'd lived all over the world growing up, I still considered Philadelphia my home city, and I'd spent a fair amount of time on the boardwalk in Wildwood. This song brought back memories.

"Night, Em!" I mouthed the words and waved.

She held up a finger in a wait-a-minute gesture and skirted the bar to come around to me. She hesitated only a minute before wrapping me in a totally-uncharacteristic-for-us hug. "Abby, I really am sorry I didn't tell you about Cooper earlier. And I promise, I won't keep that kind of secret again. I just want you to know that you can talk to me. About anything." She pointed to the ceiling, grinning. "Now that you're living upstairs, I'll be like your own personal bartender. Add that to being your friend, and I'm the perfect listening ear."

I patted her arm. "Thanks, Emmy. I'll keep that in mind." I managed a smile. "Have a good night tonight. If you need anything, just call or . . . I don't know, knock three times on the ceiling or something."

"Will do. Good night, Ab."

When I'd told Emmy that the music and noise from the bar

downstairs wouldn't bother me, it was all conjecture. This was actually my first weekend living here above the Riptide. The restaurant closed at five Sundays through Thursdays, so tonight would be the test; on Fridays and Saturdays, under Emmy's management, the busy beachfront diner morphed into the most popular dance club in the area.

Moving up here had made sense. When Jude and Logan first approached me a few months back about taking on management of their new venture at the Riverside, I'd jumped at the opportunity. I loved the Hawthorne House; it had been the perfect place for me to both recover after the debacle in Boston and to spread my wings a little. For the first time, I'd been in charge. Yes, Jude and Logan were the owners, but they trusted me. I made the day-to-day decisions, kept everything running and turned that sweet little house into a bed-and-breakfast that was booked six months out. Hawthorne House gave me back confidence I'd feared was gone forever and helped me find a measure of peace.

But after two years, I was getting restless. I didn't want to leave Crystal Cove; I'd made friends and built up a small community of people I liked and trusted. Unfortunately, there wasn't much room for growth or change at the B&B. My only options were moving or staying. Neither felt exactly right.

So when Jude came into the kitchen at the Hawthorne, raving about the old hotel she'd spotted from the river, my heart had leaped. I hadn't said anything right away, but I hadn't had to. Jude and Logan told me that they wanted me to consider not only running the place, but making it my own. I could oversee all the repairs and renovations. I'd work with Logan on the plans, tossing out to him my wildest ideas and figuring out what made sense, what didn't. Best of all, taking on the Riverside meant I could stay in Crystal Cove. Indefinitely.

In other words, it was my dream come true.

The only fly in the ointment was timing. Logan felt that I needed to focus solely on the Riverside even before it was open. The process of putting together a resort like this was involved; not only would I be in charge of making decisions about design and the physical building, I also had to coordinate the interior decoration, all the details of the spa and restaurant, the website, the point of sale computers . . . it was mind boggling. Clearly I wouldn't be doing all of that personally, but I was still the one in charge. Trying to run the Hawthorne while I was knee-deep in the Riverside prep just wasn't practical.

So while I was reluctant to give up the sweet yellow house on the main drag in the Cove, I had to agree that their plan made sense. When I'd met Alex and Cal, I felt even better. From the minute they stepped into the B&B, I knew they belonged there. As soon as the two of them agreed to take over, everything began to move fast. Suddenly, they were talking about re-doing the small set of rooms that had been my home for the past two years and making plans to move to Florida. As I listened to Alex and Cal over dinner at Jude and Logan's home, my face must've reflected the panic I was feeling.

Jude leaned over, smiling as she sipped her wine. "Abby, don't worry. We've thought about this. Logan and I wondered if you might want to move into the apartment above the Tide—temporarily, of course. When the Riverside is ready, you can have your own space there. But for the time being, would you mind living over the shop, so to speak?"

I'd seen the small apartment a few times. I knew a little about its history: Jude's grandparents had put it in above their beach-front eatery. Generations of the family had lived there at one time or another, including Jude and her late husband Daniel after they were first married. When their son Joseph had found himself with an unexpected wife and baby a few years ago, he and his wife Lindsay had moved upstairs and taken over some of the management of the Riptide.

Now that Jude was married to Logan and living in his beautiful home, Joseph, Lindsay and their two little ones had moved into Jude's old house. That left the apartment empty just in time for me to move in.

It wasn't anything grand. There was a tiny living room with an ancient sofa and scarred coffee table, a miniscule kitchen, and a bedroom that looked out over the ocean and had an attached bath. Luckily for me, I'd grown up in compact spaces; the suites my family had occupied at various hotels throughout the country were elegant and opulent, but huge they were not. I knew I could make this space work.

I hadn't thought about the Friday and Saturday nights when I'd agreed to stay here, though. And just as Emmy had warned me, it was loud. The wooden floor vibrated beneath my feet, and I could hear Gritt's voice as though he was standing next to me. Laughter and the sound of clinking glasses drifted up the steps. And although there were easily a hundred people just below me, I felt inexplicably and suddenly lonely.

Being alone wasn't something I dreaded. I'd been a solitary child; even after my sister was born when I was seven, she and I had tended to co-exist peacefully and separately. Jessica was more of a chatterbox than I was, but she rarely bothered me. Instead, I'd hear her talking to the staff, to housekeeping or to anyone else who'd listen.

And then when I was thirteen and Jess was six, my parents had very suddenly divorced. It was civilized, like everything else in our lives. One afternoon, my mother asked us to come into the dining room of our suite. We were living in San Francisco at the time; I remembered looking out over the fog-shrouded skyline as my father spoke.

He told us that he and my mother had decided they would both be happier living apart. Mom was tired of moving from city to city every few years. She was buying a house here in California, and Jess and I would stay with her.

"But you'll come to me on school holidays, and we'll have fun then." No matter how many places we'd lived and how long it had been since he'd left his homeland, my dad always carried a bit of Ireland in his voice. He glanced at my sister and me, and I detected a glimmer of uncertainty and perhaps even regret in his green eyes.

It was that flash of emotion, that small moment, that made up my mind. I turned to face my mother, who'd remained seated at the head of the table as my father paced around the room, talking.

"I don't want to stay in California."

She frowned and brushed her blonde hair out of her face. "Abby, what do you mean? You love California. And wait until you see the house I've found for us. It's near the

34

beach, so you'll like that, and you and Jess can go to the same school until you graduate. You can make friends."

"I have friends."

"Friends you won't have to leave after two years. You don't know how much you're going to enjoy that."

"I don't care. I don't want to stay here instead of moving. I don't want to leave Daddy." I crossed my arms over my chest.

Silence fell on the room. Jess glanced from our mother to me, confusion etched on her face. My dad leaned on a chair, clutching the gleaming wood until his knuckles whitened. He looked at me steadily, but I couldn't read his eyes.

"Abby." Mom reached toward me, resting one slim hand on my elbow. "I know this is difficult for you. But your father and I have discussed it, and we both feel it's better for you girls to stay in one place, with me."

I bit down on my bottom lip. "But I don't want to do that, and it's not fair that you're making me. I never complained about moving. I like living in our hotels, and I like being with Daddy. Why should I have to stay with you if I don't want to?" I sucked in a deep breath. "I'm not a baby. I should get to decide for myself."

"Abigail." My mother's voice sharpened. "You may not be a baby, but you're a long way from being a grown-up. While I understand how upsetting this is for you, in the long run—"

"Brooke." My father interrupted her, bracing against the chair until he stood straight. "Maybe Abby has a point."

Mom's mouth dropped open a little. "Colin, we went over this. We agreed that this was for the best."

"No, you agreed. I went along with it, for your sake. But if Abby doesn't want to make this change, I'm thinking we shouldn't force her."

"She doesn't know what she wants. She's not old enough to make that determination." My mother pushed back her chair. "We had an agreement, Colin."

"Why does it have to be all one way or the other? I'm not saying you're wrong, Brooke, and I'm not saying I'm right. God knows I've been wrong enough lately." He sighed and rubbed his forehead. "I'm only saying, why not give it a try? If Abby changes her mind, there's nothing to stop her from moving in with you. Nothing is written in stone here, is it?"

My mother frowned, but I could sense her wavering. "I don't know. I suppose . . ." She looked up at me, her blue eyes searching mine. "Abby, are you sure? I mean, I can call you every day. You can come visit at our new house, and maybe you'll like it."

I nodded. "Maybe. But right now, I want to stay with Daddy." I set my chin and focused on the very top of the Golden Gate Bridge. I could just barely see it, poking out above the clouds. If I kept my eyes on that, I didn't have to look at Jessica, at the hurt and the pain I knew I'd see there.

Even now, twenty years later, guilt rose up in my throat. I hated that I'd hurt my little sister. I hated that I'd caused my mother pain and doubt, particularly when I'd discovered, three years after that terrible day, what had finally caused her to leave my father. On the surface, everything in our family was fine now. I saw my mother and my sister one or two times a year, and we spoke now and then. But I knew that deep down, they'd never really forgiven me for choosing my father over them.

My cell phone buzzed, vibrating against the table where I'd left it. I leaned over to look at the screen, sighing a little when I saw my father's name on the incoming call notification.

I was tempted to ignore it. I'd had a long day, and Christ almighty, I'd just come back from spending two days dealing with my dad and all his issues. But in the end, I picked it up and hit the answer button.

"Abby, darlin'." His words slurred, and my heart sank.

"Dad, what's up?" I didn't even make an attempt to hide my impatience.

"Darlin', why must something be the matter for a father to want to talk with his beloved daughter?" As always, when Dad was in his cups, as he called it, the Irish was strong. It was as though the whiskey carried the accent along with it.

"I guess that's just how it seems lately." I dropped my head to the back of the sofa and closed my eyes. "And the fact that you saw me this morning before I left. And you might remember, maybe, promising me that things were going to change. Does any of that ring a bell?"

"Of course. And they will change. But it was only tonight, Mr. Humphries had his retirement dinner. You remember Mr. Humphries? He's worked here in Philadelphia since you were a tiny thing. Used to tote you on his shoulder through the lobby. So of course I had to be there and have a bit of a drink with him."

"Hmmm." I wasn't going to argue with my father, not tonight and not over the telephone. "Did you call Lisel, as we discussed?"

"I . . ." He trailed off, and I knew he was either trying to remember our talk about his current estranged wife or attempting to come up with a reason why he hadn't called her yet. "I haven't, no. Today was a bit busy, and then you know, the more I thought about it, shouldn't she be the one calling me? I'm not the one who walked out."

I used my free hand to massage my forehead. "No, you were the one who humiliated her in front of all her friends and yours. Coming into a dinner party completely trashed, acting like a jackass. I would've walked out on you, too."

"No, you wouldn't. Not my sweet Abby. You're the one who never left your old dad, not when your mother left, when Jessica went with her . . . you were the one who stayed. I never forget that, Abigail. I never do."

A pang of regret and sorrow gripped my heart. "Sometimes I think I didn't do you any favors that day. If I'd gone with Mom and Jess, maybe you would've gotten help. Or maybe things would be different." Would my life have been different, too? Probably. I'd often wondered what it would've been like to grow up in one place, after all.

"Never say it, Abby. If you'd left me, too, I don't know what I would've done."

"Hmm. I guess you would've kept sleeping with every willing female who crossed your path, or you would've figured out a better way to get by. By staying, I let you maintain the illusion a little longer."

"Such a low opinion you have of your old man. Wasn't there any good that came of you staying with me?" He sounded wistful, and I knew that we were now entering the self-pity portion of tonight's entertainment.

"Of course there was. You've always been a good father, to me at least. And you're an excellent business man. You taught me more about the hotel business than I could ever hope to remember. I just worry about you. The drinking . . . Dad, it's got to stop. Your doctor said—"

"Pah." Dad spat out the word. "She doesn't know what she's talking about. My family is very long-living. You remember your grandmother Abigail, God rest her soul. You were named for her. She lived to be ninety-six. "

"Granny didn't drink her weight in whiskey, either." I knew this conversation. It was destined to go in a circle until one of us finally gave up. Tonight, that was going to be me. "Look, Dad, I'm exhausted. I had that early flight, and then I hit the ground running here. Not that you've asked, but I was over at the Riverside this afternoon, checking it out. It's going to be an amazing hotel. I hope you'll come see it once we're open."

"We'll see." I heard the thread of petulant sulk. "I still don't understand why the daughter I trained up to take over my company chose to go work in the backwater wilds of Florida. Two years you wasted at a second-class inn. And now you're up to your ears in renovating some run-down old place. You could have the management of any of my hotels, you know that."

"I don't want to manage any of your properties, and we've been through this. I screwed up in Boston. You were very gracious about it, Dad, but as horrible as that was, it made me realize that I need to make my own way. I don't want to be Colin Donavan's daughter for the rest of my career. I want people to know I made it on my own merits, not just because of who you are."

"Absolute bullshit. You'll never go anywhere, hiding down in the hinterlands. I understand you needed to lick your wounds, but this is ridiculous."

"I'm not licking my wounds." Patience had left the building. "I'm establishing my own name and career. You're just upset that you can't control me anymore. Well, that's over, Dad. I love what I'm doing. I've loved making the Hawthorne House successful, and I can't wait to get to work on the Riverside. If you can't see that, well, I'm sorry, but you'll have to adjust your expectations." My finger hovered over the button that would end this exercise in futility, but I managed one more parting shot. "And don't drunk dial me anymore. It's pathetic. Call Lisel. She's your wife, and she's the one you should be talking to."

"But Abby—"

I hung up and tossed the phone to the end of the sofa, where it bounced and landed on its face. In a fit of adolescent-style pettiness, I covered it with one of the throw pillows so that even if Dad called back, the sound would be muffled.

I stalked into the bathroom and turned on the faucets in the claw foot tub. Between the sound of the gushing water and the music pulsating from below me, there was no way I'd hear a ringing phone. And I was perfectly okay with that.

I tore off my clothes with less precision and more venom than usual, throwing them into the wicker basket in the corner. This day had been frustrating from beginning to end. All I'd wanted to do was get back to the Cove, take a little peek at my new hotel, and then hide in my apartment so I'd be ready to get back to work. But no. First my visit to the Riverside had been hijacked by that cocky contractor—in the privacy of my head I refused to call him anything else. And then my father had taken away what little peace I had left with his drunken call. Men.

As I sank into the hot bath, I wondered if it was too late for me to become a nun. Preferably at a convent where fathers—and contractors— weren't allowed to call or visit.

chapter three

Ryland

"SO HOW'S CRYSTAL COVE TREATING YOU?" Cooper Davis sifted through the pile of papers I'd brought over, detailing what we needed in the way of wood working at the Riverside. He scanned each page, frowning and then nodding.

"So far, so good." I rubbed the back of my neck and glanced around the shop. I'd been in Cooper's workspace twice now, and each time it took me back to my grandfather's basement in New Jersey. The smell of the wood, the sawdust beneath my feet and the whine of the sander . . . it was all familiar. Gramps had introduced me to the beauty of working with my hands and bringing something old and potentially lost back to life. Being here, in this shed full of projects, tools, machines and lumber, reminded me of those days.

"Yeah?" Cooper stacked the papers, tapping them onto the workbench to line them up. "Is the house okay for you?"

"Oh, it's great, thanks. If you could see some of the places I've lived during projects, you'd know your house is a palace. I really appreciate it."

"Not a problem, man. It makes me feel better to know someone's on site to make sure nothing happens here at the workshop. Not that I expect anyone to bother with it, but now that I've moved out, I'm glad you'll be around, just in case."

I shrugged. "I'm a light sleeper and decent with a baseball bat if it ever came to scaring someone off. Can't promise much more than that."

"And that's all I need." He glanced at the top paper. "Have you run all these plans by Abby yet?"

I scowled. That was the only word for the reaction that woman brought out in me. "Some. Not all. Why?"

Cooper raised one eyebrow as he studied me. "Because some of what you have here doesn't jive with things she said to me. The stables? Pretty sure she wanted to make that the spa, right? And the molding and decorative wood in the bathrooms—we'd talked about using a mildew-proof composite rather than what was in there originally."

"Yeah, well, *Ms. Donavan* and I've been butting heads for two weeks now, over everything from how many steps should be leading up to the front porch to which French doors in the dining area actually stay doors. I decided to take a pass this time on hearing why what I need to do for the restoration is 'utterly impossible.'" I mimicked her tone and put air quotes around the words.

Coop grinned. "I take it you and Abby aren't exactly bosom buddies yet?"

"Yet? Try never. God, she's just the most irritating, frustrating woman and—" I stopped speaking abruptly. "And I keep forgetting what a small town this is. She's a friend of yours, isn't she? Please don't tell me she's like your sister or your cousin or something."

"No, she's not related to me. Abby's a Cove transplant, you know. She's only lived in town for a couple of years. Moved down here from . . . Philadelphia, I think. Or Boston? Somewhere up there." He waved his hand to indicate a vague northern direction.

"That makes sense. She doesn't come across like a girl who grew up in the south. She's all uptight and demanding."

"Yeah, where'd you grow up, Ryland?" One side of Cooper's mouth curled, and I sighed.

"Okay, yeah, I'm from up there, too. But I got my ass down here as soon as I could. The chicks in the South are just different. Softer. Not so grating or demanding. Why're you laughing?"

"Because you just fell into the classic trap of Southern womanhood, my friend. You let them pull you in with their—what did you call it? Softness? And then they make you think you're getting your own way, and by the time you figure out you're doing exactly what they wanted in the first place, it's too late."

"Is that what happened with you? I met Emmy. She seemed like a straight-shooter to me."

The smirk on Cooper's face morphed into something entirely different. "Emmy . . . no. She's not like that. There's not a manipulative bone in that woman's body. She'll come right out and tell you what she needs, and if you can't make it happen, she will. She's a go-getter, my girl is." His eyes took on an expression that I'd only seen once or twice in my life. "But she's still got that Southern softness. She doesn't demand. She doesn't insist. She's just . . . Emmy."

My chest tightened, and I felt a surge of something akin to jealousy, which was ridiculous because while I'd liked Emmy when I met her, she definitely wasn't my type. And the idea of having a regular girlfriend, one woman in my life, hadn't crossed my mind in a long time. The way I lived, there wasn't room for a long-distance relationship, and I'd yet to meet the woman who'd agree to tag along with me as I moved around the country.

"Maybe you got the last good one, brother."

Cooper shrugged. "It's possible, I guess. God knows I took long enough finding her. But hey, try to give Abby a fair chance."

I snorted. "Believe me, I've tried. She just has this . . . I don't know, attitude or something. Like she knows more than me and I'm wasting her time by arguing. She won't even listen to me. I think she waits every day to find out what I'm going to suggest and then comes up with a reason why it won't work."

"That doesn't sound like Abby. Maybe it's just a matter of getting to know her better. Try talking about something that doesn't have to do with the hotel. I know she can be a little demanding, but she's really good at her job."

"A *little* demanding? I told you, she's a freaking nightmare."

Cooper lifted one eyebrow. "That seems a tad harsh. I don't claim to know Abby that well, but she's probably Emmy's closest friend. And Em's an excellent judge of character. So Abby can't be that bad."

I swallowed back the answer I wanted to give. After all, as I'd said earlier, the Cove was a small town, and even though Abby Donavan was a transplant, she'd been here longer than I had. And given that she had the job running the hotel after I'd finished restoring it, chances were she was going to stick around longer than I would. I wasn't going to win any popularity contests by criticizing her, no matter how sympathetic Cooper might seem to be.

"You're probably right. I'll try to get to know her better. Could be she's nervous about the new job or something. Wants to make sure she does it all the way Logan and Jude want."

"There's no doubt Abby's a perfectionist. Some of the guys who worked for her at the bed and breakfast said she was their toughest boss ever. But they also seemed to respect her. They wouldn't do that if she was just a bully."

I forced a smile. "Thanks, Cooper. I'll keep that in mind." I pointed to the papers still in his hand. "If there's anything in the plans that look off to you, let me know. Otherwise, I'll have a discussion with Abby and get back to you about what we decide."

Cooper grinned. "You do that, Ryland. I'll be interested to see how it works out for you."

I gave him a quick wave as I left the workshop, fighting

off a sinking feeling that Coop already knew the outcome of any discussion I might have with Abigail Donavan.

Up until now, all of my interaction with the formidable Ms. Donavan (I always thought of her that way, in the privacy of my head) had taken place on the project site. I did my best to steer our more heated discussions—read: bitter arguments— away from where my crew happened to be working that day. For one thing, I didn't want them to hear the boss—and that was me, no matter what the lady might think—having his authority challenged. And for another, the last thing I needed was ribbing about this chick and her uptight attitude. I knew work crews; once they saw a weakness, they'd never let me forget it.

Today, though, knowing I was heading into a blow-up for sure, I decided to go see Abigail at her office. I'd intentionally avoided seeing her this morning; she ran like clockwork, and her typical routine included a brief stop at the hotel first thing in the morning. I'd chosen to linger at my borrowed house with the excuse that I had to talk to Cooper, knowing full well that I'd miss Her Royal Highness. But now that I'd decided to bite the bullet and confront her, I steered my truck away from the river and instead headed toward the bridge that led to Elson.

Logan had told me that his manager was using an office in his building for the time being, until we had space finished for her at the hotel. I'd been to Logan's architectural firm a few times when we were finalizing contracts for the Riverside. It was housed in a white two-story structure at the base of the bridge, making it convenient to the heart of Crystal Cove but easily accessible to the larger mainland town of Elson.

The large parking lot in front was nearly full, but I managed to find a spot in the shade. Inside, the décor of the building was simple, but refined; there were four offices on the first floor, including one belonging to an attorney and another to an accountant, while the last two housed a title company and real estate broker respectively. I knew Logan liked having these professionals under his proverbial and literal ceiling, since he patronized them all under the company he and Jude owned.

I stood for a minute at the base of the wide steps in the center of the open foyer. I'd never thought of myself as chicken shit, but I wasn't looking forward to facing Abigail Donavan. What I'd told Cooper was true; she frustrated and annoyed the crap out of me. I didn't have issues working with women. Hell, I loved chicks, and I respected anyone, man or woman, who had knowledge and ability. There wasn't a doubt in my mind that Ms. Donavan knew her job. She was smart, savvy, and I'd noticed that she treated my crew with deference. She didn't look down her aristocratic nose at them, and oddly enough, they all seemed to love her. I just didn't understand how it was that everyone else got along with Abigail, but I couldn't.

"Can I help you?" The voice that jarred me from my brooding was low and feminine, with just a hint of the South in it. "Are you lost? Or just deciding?"

The woman stood at the doorway to my left, next to a sign with black lettering that read ATTORNEY AT LAW. Her light brown hair was pulled up into one of those bun deals some girls like, and she wore a dress that skimmed her body without looking trashy. It hit just above her knees, showing off legs that made me take another long glance.

"Not lost. Just trying to figure out if I really want to go up there."

She smiled, and I noticed her eyes were a pretty light blue. "Do you have an appointment with Logan? He's a nice guy. Nothing to be scared about."

I laughed. "Yeah, if I were going up to see Logan, I'd already be there. No, I have to deal with someone else. Someone who works for him. And she *is* a little scary."

"Do you mean Abby Donavan? She's the only other person with an office up there right now. Why don't you like her? I've met her a few times, and she's lovely."

"To you, sure." I sighed. "To everyone else in the world, she's a spoonful of spun sugar. To me, she's uber-bitch."

The woman's eyes widened. "Wow."

Wincing, I rubbed my neck. "Sorry. That was harsh. We're working on the same project, a hotel rehab, and we don't always see eye-to-eye on all the decisions. I have to go up there right now and try to convince her to agree to something she doesn't want to do. That's why I'm dragging my feet." Sticking out my hand, I put on my best charming grin. "I'm Ryland Kent, by the way."

"Elizabeth Hudson." She slid her fingers alongside mine, gave a quick squeeze and stepped back. "This is my office."

"Oh, you're the lawyer."

"Guilty." She laughed. "Has my reputation preceded me?"

"Nah." I leaned against the newel post. "Logan just mentioned he'd rented out this office to an attorney. Another attorney, I guess I should say, since I hear the guy who used to have your office skipped town to find himself."

"That's what I heard, too. I didn't know him." She lifted one slim shoulder. "His loss was my gain, since I'd been looking for a new place. My old office was in the middle of Elson, and I wanted something closer to the Cove."

"Are you from here?" She didn't sound like it. Most of the natives to this area had a different accent. Elizabeth's sounded closer to how Linc spoke.

"Not originally. Mostly I grew up in Tennessee." She didn't seem inclined to say more on that topic. "I've been in this area for a few years now."

"Well, that's convenient. Just so happens I'm brand-new in town and looking for someone to show me around."

"Ryland?"

My head jerked around, as Elizabeth and I both looked up the steps. Abigail stood at the top of the staircase, one hand on the railing. From this distance, I was struck for the first time that she really was kind of hot. Most of the time, I was too tied up listening to her gripe and argue to pay attention to her face and her body, but now, from this angle, she seemed . . . more vulnerable. Less of the ice queen and more of the pretty princess.

"Hey, uh . . . Ms. Donavan." I wanted to call her Abby, as I'd heard everyone do, but I couldn't do it, not even after she'd just used my own name for the first time. She'd sounded so uncertain, surprised to see me and maybe a little taken aback at finding me chatting up the lovely Elizabeth.

"Mr. Kent." She was recovering, drawing up her body the way I'd seen before, when she was trying to make herself look taller. "I assume you're here to see me?" Her eyes flickered to Elizabeth and back to me.

"Yep." I quirked one eyebrow at the attorney and sketched a salute. "Nice to meet you, Elizabeth. Hope to see you around town."

"Same here." She glanced up at Abigail. "Hey, Abby. Love those shoes."

"Thanks." There was a definite chill in the word, but Elizabeth only smiled again, waved at me and disappeared back into her office.

I climbed the stairs, feeling the weight of Abigail's eyes on me with each step. When I'd made it all the way up, she moved back and pointed down the hall. "My office is this way."

I gave her a little bow. "Lead the way."

She hesitated only a split second before turning and walking away. I noticed that today, she was dressed in a short skirt that flared about mid-thigh as she moved. The material clung to her ass, giving me teasing glimpses of its roundness. It made me want to . . .

No. I frowned, mentally kicking myself. I wasn't interested in the princess, even if she'd seemed to thaw a little today. Sure, she had a decent body. Yeah, there was some sex appeal there. Being a man, I couldn't help how I reacted to a female. It didn't mean I was attracted to her at all. It was just biology.

"I must have missed you today at the site." Abigail opened a door and stepped inside a small room. I followed her, dropping into a chair while she skirted the desk and sat down in the only other seat.

"Yeah." I sprawled, leaning back and propping one ankle over the other. "I needed to run some of the plans by Cooper, so I just waited at the house until he came into the workshop for the day."

Her forehead wrinkled as her brows drew together. "What plans?"

"What we're going to need as far as custom woodwork. At least, the beginning."

Abigail rested her elbows on the desk and templed her fingers. "So you went to Cooper with these plans before you spoke to me."

"These didn't involve you. They're just standard stuff."

"Oh, really? Well, why don't you show them to me, and I'll make that call?"

I shrugged. "Sure, whatever." Leaning forward, I braced my feet on the floor and reached into my back pocket to pull out the folded papers. Abigail sighed and shook her head as she picked them up from the desk.

"I'm surprised you didn't just stuff them into your shirt." She smoothed the wrinkles.

"Sorry, fancy leather briefcases aren't my style."

"How about just a manila folder? That too high-class for you?" I watched her eyes as she scanned the top paper. Well-manicured fingernails slid beneath it to flip through the rest of the plans. Her jaw tensed, lips pressed together, and it might've been my imagination, but I almost thought I saw steam coming out of her ears. When she spoke, fury laced her voice.

"Are you insane or just incompetent?" Abigail pushed the pile away, as though she might be able to make them all disappear. "I didn't approve any of this, and I know for a fact that Logan didn't either. You seem to be under the impression that you're in charge here, Mr. Kent, and I'm here to tell you that you're wrong." She snatched at the plans she'd just pushed away, spreading them until she found what she wanted. "'Restoring the barns to their original condition and purpose.' What the hell? Those barns are going to be the spa, and you know it. We've discussed it. I told you to draw permits for plumbing and electric out there. I'm assuming that hasn't been done."

I gritted my teeth. "No. I think we should revisit the idea of the spa—"

"I'm sure you do, but it's not going to happen. Offering those services is an integral part of our business plan."

"But the hotel didn't originally have a spa. It had barns."

She slammed her hand down onto the desk, hard, and I jumped. I'd never seen her this worked up. Normally when we disagreed, Abigail got colder and stiffer. Her words got longer and more convoluted. She'd never been this physical, this . . . heated.

"Of course it didn't have a spa. It had barns because people used horses when it was built. That was then, and this is now. And now, the Riverside Hotel *and Spa* will damn well have a spa. Are we clear, Mr. Kent?" She was practically spitting.

"I don't think it needs to be that cut and dried. Why can't this be discussed?"

"Because it's not your call. Logan, Jude and I made the decision long before they brought you on board." Abigail pushed her chair back, jumped to her feet and paced in the small space behind her desk. "Tell me something, Mr. Kent. Do you always hijack your—your *restorations*? When you rebuilt the Colton farmhouse in Virginia and they changed it from a home to a winery, did you try to change their minds? When you did that place in Kansas City and they opened a bar in it rather than keeping it a smithy, did you pitch a fit?"

I shifted in my seat, uncomfortable. The truth was, I hadn't cared about those places. I'd known from the get-go what the owners planned to do, and I'd adjusted my restoration accordingly. I'd brought kitchens up to modern specs, adjusted window sizes and changed door locations without blinking. So why was this job any different?

"The Riverside's special. She's been neglected so long, and I just need to do right by her." I braced, waiting for more venom, but it didn't come.

Abigail stopped abruptly in mid-pace. She stared at me, blinking rapidly, her bottom lip caught between her teeth. For the space of several breaths, she didn't speak.

"Don't you think I want the same thing?" Her words were tired, almost exasperated, but not angry anymore. "Don't you think I see the potential, too? But I'm a business-woman. I know that in this day and age, it takes more than a faithful restoration and a lovely hotel to keep guests coming in. People say they love charm and history and all that, but when it comes down to it and they have to decide between us and the chain motel out on the main strip in Elson, there has to be another hook. The spa is part of that hook, along with the restaurant and the boating activities. Those are what will pay to keep up the historical accuracy and charm that're so important to you."

She was right. I knew it, and I felt like a jerk for going around her to try to get my own way. It'd never happened before, and now I had to grovel. I hated groveling.

"I'm sorry, Abigail. You're on target, and I shouldn't have talked to Cooper before I'd discussed it with you."

She kept her gaze steady on me for a few more minutes, assessing. "Thank you."

"Is that it? You're not going to yell at me more, rub it in that I was a dick?"

Her lips twitched, but she shook her head. "There's nothing to be gained by doing that. You admitted you were wrong, you apologized. Let's move on." She chewed the corner of her lip. "I saw you had something on there about using real wood trim in the bathrooms. Is that really cost-effective? Or will we end having to replace it all the time? The composite I'd intended to use is supposed to be mildew-resistant."

I realized she was extending an olive branch. I'd screwed up, and she had every right to ream me out, maybe even go to Logan about what I'd done. But instead she was offering a compromise. I took a deep breath.

"The composite won't mildew, probably, but it's also not going to be as durable. You have people coming in and out of these rooms, and there's going to be wear and tear. With the composite, you'll see dents, nicks and chips—a lot of them, and pretty much right away. I suggested the solid wood to minimize that factor. If you're worried about mildew, why not put on a special sealant? It can be reapplied easily as needed, and you'll still have the strength of the wood."

"I'm always worried about mildew. This is Florida, and humidity is a killer." Abigail tapped her lips, her eyes on the desk. "Okay. I'm willing to concede to real wood trim throughout, provided it's sealed."

"Done." I stood up, too, stretching my back as I felt the tension draining away. "I'll let Cooper know, and I'll give him the changes about the barns, too. I mean, the spa." I retrieved the papers from the top of her desk and folded them up again. "And I'll call the county today about those permits."

"Thanks. I appreciate it." Abigail gripped the back of her office chair, and her shoulder sagged a little. I guessed the stress of this meeting had sapped her energy, just as it had mine. A thread of guilt cinched my chest.

"Look at that." I made an attempt at a teasing grin. "We just worked something out without either of us completely losing our shit. There might be hope for this project yet."

She shot me a look of wry disbelief, one eyebrow raised. "First of all, I don't 'lose my shit'. I'm a professional, and this is my job. You don't have to like me, Mr. Kent, but I'll be damned if you don't at least respect what I can do."

I stuck one hand in my pocket and waited for the rest. One thing I'd learned was that if Abigail Donavan started a sentence with 'first of all', there had to be at least a second, and often, even a third and fourth.

"Second of all . . ." *Yep, there it was.* "Working something out between two people who care about what they do should be the rule, not the exception. I'm still not clear on exactly why you feel the need to take the opposite stand on anything I suggest. But as you said, today was a good step. Maybe we can use what we learned to make sure things run more smoothly from here on out."

I wasn't sure how she'd done it, but this woman had just twisted my words and put me in my place at the same time as she'd agreed with me. At least partially. I had no idea how to respond, so I just nodded and turned to leave.

"Thanks for coming by, Mr. Kent."

I paused at the doorway, glancing back over my shoulder. "You know, the gig's up on that, right?"

She frowned. "On what?"

"I know you know my name. You called me Ryland out there on the steps."

Her pale cheeks took on just the hint of a pink glow, but she didn't answer me.

"I'm just saying. It wouldn't make you less in charge or make anyone think less of you if you called me Ry every now and then." I dropped my voice, giving it just the slightest edge of intimacy. "Maybe even if it's just when we're alone."

She swallowed, and her lips pressed together again. I was making her uncomfortable, but even then, she wasn't willing to let me have the last word.

"I'll try to keep that in mind." One side of her mouth curved just a little, and I spied a dimple I'd never noticed before. "Mr. Kent."

I couldn't help it. I laughed and shook my head. *Yeah,*

she was still the ice queen.

But I was whistling as I strode down the steps and out to my truck.

chapter four

Abby

FOUR WEEKS INTO THE RIVERSIDE remodel, my days had taken on a fairly steady routine. I woke up each morning in my small apartment, showered and dressed before heading downstairs for coffee, brewed either by Jude or by her son, Joseph. If Jude was behind the bar, I was more likely to linger. I didn't know Joseph as well, of course, though I knew a little bit of his story from Emmy. She'd told me how he'd left college when his father was very ill, so that Jude didn't have to handle everything on her own. When he'd gone back, a little over a year later, it was to discover that Lindsay, the girl he'd been casually dating, had given birth to their child during Joseph's absence.

Joseph might've been surprised, but he stepped up. He

and Lindsay had gotten married, moved to Crystal Cove and begun helping Jude run the Tide. They'd moved into her old house shortly before the birth of their daughter Brenna last year. Joseph was close to graduating—he was only going to college part-time, so that he could work—and I knew Jude was proud of her son's dedication and responsibility. He was always kind and courteous to me, greeting me with a smile and sometimes a story about his son DJ's latest antics.

My first stop of the day, after coffee, was always at the job site. I was excited every morning to see what progress had been made the day before; sometimes it was very little visible to my eye, but on other days, walls had been taken down or repaired, new sections of the hotel opened for me to examine or windows replaced. I tried to check in with Ryland every day, to make sure we both stayed on the same page. It wasn't that I didn't trust him, not really; after he'd tried to go around me on the spa, we'd both been treating each other with a little more caution and deference. I just felt it was prudent to keep an eye on all the details so that there weren't any more snafus.

I was dragging my feet this morning, though. I hadn't slept well, and once I had dropped off, I'd been so deeply asleep that the alarm didn't wake me up. Since I wasn't meeting with any vendors or other professionals today, I gave myself permission to wear jeans and a sleeveless blouse instead of a skirt or dress, and I pulled my hair into a high pony tail.

The day immediately got a little better when I saw Jude behind the bar. She was standing with her back to me, staring out at the beach as the sun rose high in the sky. She turned around as I closed the door to my staircase behind me.

"Good morning, sunshine." Jude smiled and unhooked a mug from the top of the rack. As I came closer, she narrowed her eyes, peered at me and shook her head. "I think it's a good thing for you that I made the coffee extra-high test this morning. You look like you could use it."

"Thanks." I eased onto a bar stool and watched her pour the coffee and slide it toward me, along with the sugar and cream. One of my few indulgences when it came to food was sweet, creamy coffee. I'd never mastered the knack of drinking it black, like my father, or even just with cream, like my mom. Holding up the cup, I inhaled deep and closed my eyes. "Mmmmm. What is it about coffee that instantly makes my morning so much better?"

Jude laughed. "Addiction, probably. But it's okay, Abby, you're allowed a few weaknesses."

I sipped, taking a few minutes to appreciate the sweet warmth. "So how was your trip? Virginia this time, right?"

"Yep." She folded a bar rag into a perfect square. "Shenandoah Valley. It was breathtaking. I fell in love."

"I bet." Ever since they'd gotten married, Logan had been stealing Jude away on short trips here and there. She'd never traveled very much before, as running the Tide was pretty much a twenty-four/seven life-long commitment. But now that Joseph and Lindsay were around to help carry the load, it was possible for her to live a little more. "We have a hotel in Richmond, and we lived there for a few months. I took a few weekends in the western part of the state."

"You've lived everywhere, haven't you?" Jude wiped at a few drops of water on the bar. "We had a wonderful time.

But Logan says he's not taking me out of the state anymore because I keep coming up with new business ideas for us wherever we go."

I smiled, shaking my head. "What was it this time? So far you two have a restaurant, a bed and breakfast, an architectural firm and a development company between you. Not to mention the hotel currently in progress, and didn't I hear something about a new restaurant down the coast a little?"

Jude winced a little. "Yeah, I know. You're right. But this could actually dovetail with all of them. We stopped at this adorable little winery in the mountains, and I said to Logan, 'Wouldn't a winery be the perfect complement to all our businesses?' You know, we could feature our wine here at the Tide, at the B&B and the Riverside, and ooooh—can you see it? We could offer packages. Come to Crystal Cove, stay at either the Hawthorne House or the Riverside Inn and take a wine tour, too."

"Jude?" I reached across the bar to lay my hand on her arm. "This, my friend, is an addiction. I can get you help. We might need an intervention."

She sighed and patted my hand. "I know. But at least my addiction makes us money, right?"

"After you spend some and we all work hard—yeah." I took another deep drink of coffee. "But if you're serious about this winery, I have someone you can talk to about it. Get some hints and so on."

"Really?" She raised one eyebrow. "I didn't know you had connections there."

I didn't quite meet her eyes. "Yes. My step-father owns a vineyard in Napa."

Jude was quiet. "I didn't even know you had a step-father. You've never mentioned him."

I shrugged. "There wasn't any need up to now. He's a nice guy, though. His name's Geoffrey Adams, and the vineyard's been in his family for generations. I'll text you his information this morning."

"Geoffrey Adams? I've heard of him." Jude leaned against the counter behind her. "You, Abby Donavan, are a woman of mystery."

I forced a smile. "Nah, I just don't like to talk about my family if I can help it. But Geoff'll tell you everything you need to know." I finished my coffee and pushed aside the empty mug. "Just don't tell Logan I hooked you up. He might kill me. Or fire me. Maybe both."

"Don't worry, your secret's safe with me." Jude folded her arms across her chest. "So how're things going at the Riverside? Logan tells me the restoration is moving along. He said the dining room is beautiful."

"It is. And Cooper's working on the final design for the banister. Once it's in, the foyer will be done, for all intents and purposes. Ryland just hired the new crew to start the guest rooms."

"I can't wait to see it all. I haven't been over there since the work started, and I was thinking of waiting until it was done, but I'm too excited. I'll try to pop in this week." She picked up my empty mug. "How about you and Ryland? Everything going smoothly there?"

I glanced down. Jude was my boss, yes, but she was also a friend. Aside from Emmy, she was probably my best friend in Crystal Cove. But although I felt perfectly comfortable complaining to Em about Ryland Kent and his cocky attitude, I knew there was a different line with Jude. I couldn't just unload on her without jeopardizing Ryland's position as well as my own. One of the first things my dad had taught me was the importance of maintaining a persona. The Abigail Donavan the world saw was poised, self-assured and capable. I didn't want to give Jude any reason to doubt my ability to handle the job she'd given me.

"Yes, everything's fine. He's good at what he does, and the men he hired are hard workers. I like the fact that he uses local talent for the basic work. Apparently his fine-tuning staff, as he calls it, is coming up in a few weeks."

"Hmmm." Jude nodded. "Cooper told me there was some kind of mix-up with the spa plans. He said you handled it, though."

Mentally I rolled my eyes. I should've known that Cooper would tell Logan and Jude about anything that might affect their property. "Oh, it was just a misunderstanding. I took care of it, and everything's set now."

"Wonderful." She retied her apron, making the knot at the back of her neck a little more secure. "You know, Ab, Logan and I did a lot of research before we hired Ryland Kent. We wanted him because he's the best in the business. He's young, sure, but his talent and reputation are better than contractors twice his age. He's got vision."

I tried not to cringe. *Had Cooper said something else? Did Ryland complain about me, either to Coop or directly to Logan?*

"That being said . . . he's a man. And I've been a working woman long enough to know that no matter how enlightened a man can be, there're times when he might try to bully a woman. He might not even realize it; some men just think their plans and ideas make more sense, so they believe they're doing us a favor by pushing for their own way. I'm not saying Ryland's doing that." Jude held up one hand as I opened my mouth. "And I'm not asking you to rat him out, or gripe about him. I know you, Abby. That's not your style. You'd grit your teeth and get through it until you'd have nothing left but bleeding gums, rather than ask for help or say someone's giving you trouble. But I want you to keep in mind that I've got your back. Logan and I believe in you. We trust *you*. And in our book, you are the final word on anything that happens at the Riverside."

It was mortifying to realize my eyes were filled with tears. I never cried. I hadn't in years, and most certainly not in any work-related situation. I was a Donavan, and Donavans were tough. I could almost hear my father's voice.

But Jude's support was more important than I'd known. Hearing her affirm that she and Logan would back me in a show-down with Ryland took a weight off my shoulders that I hadn't realized I was carrying. I swallowed hard and raised my eyes to meet Jude's.

"Thank you. Really, you have no idea how much that means to me. You and Logan have been my lifesavers these past few years, and I don't know what I would've done without you." I let a moment of silence pass as I collected myself. "But everything's fine with the contractor. I can hold my own. And I think he gets that now."

"I'm sure he does." Jude's voice held more than a trace of amusement. "I can't see anyone getting the better of you,

Abby. Ryland's a good guy, I think. Cooper likes him, and that speaks volumes, since Coop doesn't really like anyone outside the posse."

I smiled. It was a long-playing joke among the group of friends that Cooper Davis didn't play well with others. He could be gruff, sure, and he didn't suffer fools. I knew that. But then, neither did I. The difference was that while Cooper was seen as being an eccentric artist, the same traits in me apparently made me a bitch. *Oh, well.*

"He's pretty cute, too." Jude added those last words with a sly glance my way. "His arms . . . wow. Well, I've got a thing for arms. And those dark eyes? Mmmmm."

I gave her wide eyes and shook my head. "Jude, you're a married woman. Really. What would Logan say?"

"He'd say I can look as long as I know whose bed I'm in every night. And I might be married, but I'm far from dead. I also happen to have some single friends, so I keep my eyes open. Ryland Kent looks like he could be a lot of fun."

I slid off the barstool. This conversation was taking a turn down a road that I'd blocked off a long time ago. There were dangerous potholes there, and I wasn't in the state of mind to navigate them this morning. "Well, good luck with that. I hope you can find the right single friend for Mr. Kent."

"I think I already did. Abby, you haven't had even one date since you moved to the Cove. At least, not as far as I know, which means you'd have to be playing it pretty close to the chest, since nothing happens in Crystal Cove without someone finding out. Why not take a second look at Ryland? Sounds like the sparks are there already."

I rolled my shoulders, trying to release the tension that

had suddenly seized them. "First of all, I'm not looking for a man. Or a relationship. Or even a one-night hookup, if you want to sound like Emmy. Second, if I were looking, it wouldn't be with anyone from work. Been there, done that, still have the scars. And third, Ryland Kent is younger than me. Considerably younger. He's not interested in someone like me. Trust me on that."

Jude sighed. "Abby, you're hardly ancient. Hell, I'm over ten years older than you and *I'm* not ancient. Ryland would be stupid not to think you're incredibly hot. As for the fact that you're not looking . . . trust me, sweetie. It happens whether you're looking or not, and more often than not, the guy you fall for isn't the one your logical brain would choose."

"And on that note, I need to get to work." I pulled out my phone to check the time. "My boss is a real stickler for punctuality, and I don't want to be late. Thanks for the coffee, Jude. See you later on."

"Don't forget to send me that info on the winery." She called the words after me, and I paused to look back, waving to show I'd heard her.

"And don't forget to check out Ryland's arms, either. His chest is pretty smokin', too. Oh and his ass—"

I clapped my hands over my ears and hummed loudly as I pushed through the swinging screen door that led to the parking lot. I probably looked ridiculous, but desperate times and all that. I didn't need the mental image of the restoration specialist's finer points haunting me all day long.

I decided to skip my early-morning visit to the site when I remembered that I was scheduled to be at the hotel in the early afternoon to meet the county plumbing inspector. Instead, I spent the morning going over the resumés we'd already received for the restaurant staff positions.

I'd culled out the obvious nos and separated the rest into piles of definite call-backs and maybes when one name stopped me dead in my tracks.

Zachary Todd.

I hadn't seen his name in a long time. I'd thought about him every day for a while, and then less often since I'd moved to the Cove. But seeing his resumé now, in black and white on my desk, took my breath away. My hands shook a little as I lifted the paper.

The last I'd heard, he was working for Ross-Holmdale, a small but well-respected hotel chain out of Memphis. It wasn't Donavan Hotels, for sure, but then again, he'd well and truly burned his bridges there. Landing the position with Ross-Holmdale was impressive, all things considered.

Which made the fact that his resumé was on my desk even odder. Why would the man who was on the cusp of running the entire restaurant branch of a successful hotel chain apply for a job at a single hotel, not affiliated with any chain or franchise? While I was excited about the Riverside, I didn't have any delusions that Jude and Logan intended it to be their flagship. They were entrepreneurs, investors, not hoteliers. Taking this position would be a definite step down for someone like Zachary whose ambition was enormous. It was certainly bigger than anything he'd felt for me.

"Abby, you asked me to remind you when it was one o'clock. It's just that now." Carolyn Jacobs, Logan's senior administrative assistant, stuck her head into my open door.

"Thanks, Carolyn. Hey, can I ask you something?"

She smiled and leaned her hip against the door jam. "Sure. What do you need?"

I laid Zachary's letter back on the pile. "You posted the listing for all the hotel jobs, didn't you? Do you know if my name was mentioned in any of those announcements?"

Carolyn cocked her head. "I wrote them all. Hmmm, no, I don't think we said anything about you specifically. Should I have?"

"No, not at all. I was just curious. One of the responders is someone I used to know, and I wondered if he was aware of my involvement." I smiled. "It's really not a big deal." I reached into the bottom drawer of my desk and grabbed my purse. "Thanks for reminding me. I'll probably head home after this meeting at the site, so I'll see you tomorrow."

I drove to the Riverside on automatic pilot, my mind stuck on Zachary and why in the world he'd want a job down here, at a hotel where there wouldn't be any opportunity for advancement. It bothered me because I didn't trust him or his motives, and not knowing what he might have up his sleeve made me feel jittery. Unsettled.

I parked in my normal spot in the gravel lot close to the river, in the front of the hotel. I heard the noise of pounding hammers and the whirl of power tools in the distance, at one of the outbuildings, but the main hotel was quiet. Making my way across the lawn, I climbed the three steps to the porch. That had been a Ryland victory; Logan's original design had shown two steps, and I'd liked the way it had looked on paper. But the restoration specialist had insisted that the hotel had been built with three stairs, and he felt it was important to the preserve that integrity. I'd given in, because what he said made sense to me. I also knew the value in giving in now and then.

My footsteps echoed in the foyer. The floors had been laid earlier in the week, and it had been the perfect touch to finish this charming, welcoming space. I stopped for a minute and turned slowly, smiling.

Across the room, there was a sound at the registration desk. I jerked my head in that direction, but no one stood there. The counter was original to the hotel. Ryland and Cooper had worked on restoring it together, and I had to admit, it was gorgeous. I made my way over there now, and the closer I drew to that corner, the more uneasy I felt. I couldn't explain exactly why, but I was sure if I turned my head fast enough, I'd see someone standing near me. It was a presence I felt, something strong and tangible.

It wasn't the only time I'd had an odd feeling here in the Riverside. The very first day I'd met Ryland, when I'd been walking the halls, for just a moment I was positive someone else had been there with me. Later I'd chalked it up to Ryland's presence, but in the back of my mind, I wasn't convinced. And more than once, I'd heard unexplained noises, seen odd movement out of the corner of my eye and felt that prickle at the back of my neck.

Of course, I didn't believe in ghosts. But at the same

time, I respected this formidable old structure and all the years it had seen. Maybe it had absorbed energies or whatever it was people seemed to think might happen. I didn't think the presence I felt was malicious; more, it seemed to me, the hotel itself was waiting with baited breath to see what Ryland and I did to bring it back to life. I desperately wanted to make it happy, as ridiculous as that sounded. I didn't want to disappoint anyone, dead or alive.

When nothing else moved or made noise, I ventured further into the building. Renovation had begun in some of the guest rooms already, and I smiled, marveling at what a difference some time and attention made. I could see what it was going to be. Nothing was finished, but the bones were there, and they were lovely indeed.

"Hey."

I whirled around, my hand flying to my throat. Ryland sat in the empty dining room across the hall from where I stood. He was sprawled over a pile of cut wood, watching me.

"My God, you scared me to death. What're you doing sitting there?"

Ryland raised one eyebrow. "Plumbing inspector called and said he'd be late. I figured you were already on your way, so I've been waiting here to tell you."

"You couldn't have sent me a text? Just decided to seize the opportunity to sit around and take it easy? And where's everyone else?"

He stared up at me, the expression on his face unreadable. "They're all working over at the barn and garages today. Nothing for them to do here until we get this plumbing signed off." He frowned, still regarding me. "You know, people say you're nice. Everyone I meet in this town, they say, 'Oh, Abby Donavan's just wonderful.' And I know you can be a decent person with my crew. I've seen you interact with vendors and subs and inspectors, and you're actually a normal human being. But with me, you can't seem to be anything but snide. Why is that, do you think?"

I regarded him for a minute, and then I sighed and bent to pull over my own pile of wood. Sitting down, I stretched out my legs. "You're right. It's just . . . I don't know. Maybe you bring out the worst in me. I see you, and it seems like all the manners and polite conversation I was ever taught fly out the window. I forget it all. I should probably apologize."

Ryland lifted one shoulder. "If you don't know why you do it, an apology wouldn't mean very much." His eyes narrowed, and he frowned. "What's wrong?"

I forced a smile. "What do you mean? Nothing's wrong."

"Yeah, there is. Your eyes look all shadowed, and your shoulders have been bunched up tense since you walked in here. What's the problem? It's got to be more than just me."

"Nothing. It's something—well, I guess it's a little more than personal, since it affects others. But it's all right. I'll deal."

"I'm sure you will." Ryland smiled, and his eyes were warm, making me remember Jude's teasing from earlier. "But maybe talking to someone like me would help."

"Someone like you? Have you added personal therapist to your list of talents?" I was trying to tease him off-course, but the man would not be deterred.

"Someone who doesn't know you. Someone who can

listen without prejudice."

I rubbed my forehead, just at the top where my hairline met skin. "If I tell you, you're probably going to think I'm stupid, or at the very least, that I have terrible judgment." I hesitated. "I haven't told anyone in the Cove about this, so if you're a blabber mouth, tell me now."

"My friends call me the vault. Once a secret comes in, it doesn't get out. Ever." He nudged my leg with his foot, the huge work boot almost knocking me over. "C'mon, Donavan. I thought we had a truce or something going. What better way to cement our friendship but with shared secrets?"

"Ha!" I laughed, in spite of myself. "So you're going to share a secret, too? I can't wait to hear this."

"Hey, I've got secrets. I'm deep, Donavan. Haven't you figured that out yet?"

I shook my head. "Whatever you say."

"So 'fess up. Tell me what's got your panties in a twist this morning."

"My panties are not in a twist. And I hate that phrase. It's demeaning."

"Why? Because it implies you wear panties?" Ryland wiggled his eyebrows at me. "Why, Ms. Abigail Donavan, are you telling me you aren't? Are you going commando?"

My face heated, and I was sure he could see the flush. "That, Mr. Kent, is none of your business."

He leaned back a little, resting his weight on his hands. "You're probably right. But you're trying to distract me. Talk to me, woman."

Most of the time, I hated being called 'woman', too. But for some reason, the way it rolled off Ryland Kent's lips didn't bother me so much. I took a deep breath. "I don't know whether you know this, but my family owns some hotels. That's how I got into the business."

He nodded. "Cooper told me you're actually one of *the* Donavans."

"*The* Donavans." I gave a short bark of laughter. "Yeah, that's me. Well, my first managing position was at our property in Boston. I was so excited, and I wanted to show my father that I had what it took to be an important part of the business. I wanted to make him proud." I paused, remembering those first heady days in New England. "And at first it was all wonderful. And then I met a man."

"Ah." Ryland's lip curled just a little. "A man."

"Yeah. His name was Zachary Todd, and he was the assistant manager of the restaurant within The Donavan Boston. The restaurants are a separate business, but they're also owned by my family. Zachary . . . he was amazing." I remembered the first time he'd spoken to me, standing close enough that I could breathe the scent he wore and feel how very male he was. When he'd taken me out to dinner, he kept his hand on my lower back with just enough pressure to make me hyper-aware of him.

"Amazing, huh? What made him so special?"

I glanced up at Ryland. I'd nearly forgotten he was still sitting with me. "Oh, I don't know. He was intense. And he focused that intensity on me. I'd never had a serious relationship before, because I'd been so single-minded about school and then my career, and I guess I was an easy target for him. My dad said he was putting the moves on me."

"Your father didn't like him?"

I snorted. "You could say that. He'd never taken much interest in my personal life up to the time I started seeing Zachary. And then suddenly he was up in Boston all the time. It felt like he didn't trust me."

Ryland shifted, but his eyes never left my face. "I assume your dad turned out to be right."

I clenched my jaw. "My father made sure he turned out to be right. You know that trite thing you see in movies where the overbearing father offers the daughter's unsuitable boyfriend an insane amount of money if he'll go away? And because the boyfriend is so madly in love with the girl, he turns it down?"

The corner of his mouth twitched, but Ryland only nodded. "Sure."

"Well, in my case, it worked. Dad offered to make Zachary vice president of the restaurant division if he'd agree to break things off with me. And Zachary jumped so fast to say yes that it made my head spin."

"Sounds like a real prince. Your father did you a favor."

I rolled my eyes. "You sound just like him. Yes, my father was right about Zachary. But how he went about it was terribly humiliating to me. My dad made me feel like an idiot for not seeing through Zachary, and then what was worse, it turned out that Zachary had been stealing from the company. Well, not out-and-out stealing, I guess, but his actions were unethical, if not criminal."

"So did he go down for that?"

This was the toughest part. "No. Zachary . . . had used me to cover up some of what he'd done. I didn't know it at the time, but if my father had pressed charges, I might've been implicated. So no, he just left the company without a recommendation. And my father replaced me."

Ryland's eyes narrowed. "He replaced you? What the hell?"

"At the Boston hotel, not as a daughter." I'd meant it as a joke, but judging from the dark look on his face, Ryland wasn't laughing.

"But why would he do that? It wasn't your fault. It was the douchebag's."

I pulled up my knees to hug them into my chest. "Yes, but I'd proven that I wasn't ready to handle a hotel on my own. I wasn't trustworthy, and I'd been taken in by Zachary. So Dad wanted to bring me back to Philadelphia, have me take a staff job until I was ready to try again. It was devastating."

"Yeah, that would be. What did you do?"

"I didn't have that many options. I'd only ever worked at Donavan Hotels, and even though I had my degree, anyone hiring me would've wanted to know why I was leaving my family business. My father's a big presence in the hotel world. Word would've gotten out that he didn't want me working anywhere else, and that would've been it."

Ryland leaned closer to me, almost as though he were going to touch my hand, but he pulled short at the last minute. "So how'd you end up in Florida?"

"I'm not entirely sure. One day just before I left Boston, I got an email, asking if I might be interested in a position managing a new bed and breakfast. It was from Logan, actually. He said they were looking for someone with experience and flexibility. I'd be totally in charge." I lifted one shoulder.

"I didn't take much time to think it over. I just . . . ran."

"Seems like you landed on your feet. You like this place, don't you? The Cove?"

I smiled. "I love the Cove. Jude and Logan are wonderful, and I've made friends. My job is exactly what I want it to be. Just when I was feeling like the B&B was getting a little too familiar, too easy, the Riverside came along." I ducked my head, hiding my face from Ryland. "That's why this place is so important to me. I know I can be a pain in the neck sometimes—"

"Sometimes? And the pain isn't in my neck, either."

"Okay, fine. I'm a raging bitch. But it's because the Riverside is pretty much my salvation. Being the manager here means I can stay in the Cove indefinitely. I don't have to go crawling back to my father or figure out how to get a job somewhere else."

This time, Ryland did touch my hand, closing his fingers over the mine. My breath hitched as the heat of his palm spread over my skin, and if I'd believed in such things, I'd have sworn my heart skipped a beat.

It's just because you haven't had a man touch you in way too long. This doesn't have anything to do with Ryland.

"You're not really a raging bitch. You're just—you're tough, Donavan. I'm honest enough to admit that if you were a guy, I wouldn't think twice about it. There's just something about a girl who acts the same way—"

"Girl?" I tilted my head. "Mr. Kent, I'm not a girl. I'm a woman."

A slow smile spread over his face. "Very true. Don't think I haven't noticed."

Before I could respond, we heard a bang coming from the front of the hotel. I jumped, and Ryland pulled away, springing to his feet.

"What was that?" I whispered the words, even though I knew there wasn't anyone around.

"Not sure." Ryland moved to stand closer to the doorway, and I realized he was putting himself between me and whatever was out there. "There've been some weird things—"

"Hey, Kent! You around here?" Tony Landoff, the county plumbing inspector, appeared in the door way. "Sorry about the delay. My truck broke down and I had to switch it out." He noticed me and whipped off the grimy old baseball cap on his head. "Hey there, Ms. Donavan. How you doing?"

"I'm fine, Mr. Landoff, thanks. Looking forward to getting this part done so we can get moving on the spa next."

"Well, let's get to work then." He turned to head for the kitchen, and Ryland made to follow.

I snagged his arm as he passed. "Hey." I kept my voice low. "Thanks for listening. I appreciate it."

"I keep telling you, Donavan, I'm a good guy." He paused, letting Tony get a little ahead of us. "You never did tell me why you were upset today. You only gave me the history."

I shrugged. "It's nothing I can't handle. I was going through resumés for the restaurant manager position here at the Riverside, and Zachary's was in the pile. It just shook me up. But I'll deal with it."

We kept walking, and I realized my hand was tucked into the crook of Ryland's elbow. It felt somehow right there.

"You're not going to interview him, are you? You threw it away, right?"

I bit the side of my lip. "I didn't throw it away, but no, I'm not that much of an idiot. Or a glutton for suffering. I'm just curious about why he'd want this job. He works for another hotel chain, and from what I've heard, he's doing well there."

Ryland growled. There wasn't any other way to describe the noise he made. "Leave it alone, Abby."

I stiffened a little. "I can take care of myself. If I decide that I want to talk to him, find out what he wants, I'll do it with my eyes wide open, believe me." I ventured a glance at Ryland's face. His eyebrows were drawn together and his eyes were darker than usual as he jerked his arm away from me.

"Fine. You handle it yourself, take care of yourself. You wouldn't want to need anyone, would you, Donavan?"

He strode forward, catching up with Tony. I stood alone in the hallway, listening to the men's voices echo from the kitchen. A cool breeze slid over my skin, carrying with it the faintest trace of lilacs. It was somehow as comforting as a mother's hug.

chapter five

Ryland

"**H**EY, BOSS. WE FINISHED THAT section of dry-wall in the east wing hall, so we're knocking off. Okay?"

I pulled my attention away from the papers in my hand. "You what? Oh, yeah. What time is it?"

The dust-covered foreman lifted off his baseball cap and ran a hand over sweat-dampened hair. "After six. We wanted to get to a good stopping place, but it's Friday, and the guys are done."

"Yeah, okay." I rolled up the papers and shoved them into the back pocket of my jeans. "You all go on ahead. See you tomorrow, Stan."

He turned to leave and then glanced back at me. "You

outta here, too? Looks like it might storm soon. There're some wicked black clouds in the east."

"In a minute. I need to check on a few things before I close up." When he hesitated, I grinned and gave him a cuff on the shoulder. "I promise, I'm not going to be long." My phone buzzed in my pocket, and lifting it up, I checked the incoming call screen. "I need to take this. You guys get out of here and enjoy your evenings."

I stepped into the nearest guest room, already dry-walled and taped up, and answered the call. "Hey, Linc. What's up?"

"What's up is that I'm going to be there tomorrow, and the rest of the finishing crew is scheduled to arrive by Monday. You ready for us?"

I turned in a slow circle, checking out the room. "Pretty much. The local guys are working a half-day tomorrow, and then they'll move to supporting our people. We're just about on schedule."

"Well, hell, imagine that. And no surprises? No cracked foundations or creeping black mold?"

"Foundation's solid. We found some spots of mold and some pretty wicked mildew, but we expected that. It's Florida. It was all taken care of. But yeah, so far, so good." I leaned against the sanded wood of the wide door way. "How were things in Texas?"

There was a long silence on the other end, and I took the phone away from my ear to make sure we hadn't been disconnected. When my friend finally spoke, his voice was rough. "Same as always. The kids are getting big. It took a while for them to warm up, but then once they did, we had a great time. They're awesome, Ry. Getting so grown-up."

I hooked my thumb in the front pocket of my jeans. "I bet. You took pictures, right?"

"Yeah, I'll show you when I get there." He was quiet again for a minute. "Leaving them almost fucking killed me, man. They cried, and they begged me not to go. It was the worst thing I've ever done."

I blew out a long breath. "Did you talk to them, Linc? To Hank and Doris? It's time, brother. There's no reason you shouldn't have those kids with you."

"Hank says with my lifestyle, it doesn't make sense for me to have custody. He asked me if I thought the best thing for my children would be yanking them out of the life they know and dragging them around the country with me." I heard his heavy sigh on the other end of the phone. "He's not wrong, Ry. They're not . . . unreasonable. They just want what's best for the kids."

"And you don't?" I ducked my head and ran my free hand through my hair. "That's bullshit, Linc. You're their father. Sylvia would want them with you."

"Yeah, well, Sylvia wouldn't have wanted me to become a drunk after she died. Doris and Hank saved my ass when they took Becca and Oliver, and they've given them structure and stability. I can't blame them for not trusting me, for thinking they can give them a better future than I ever could. It just . . . it kills me when they cry."

I swallowed, remembering. Linc and Sylvia had been married when I'd met them, and Rebecca had been a baby. She'd been an adorably chubby angel, all blonde hair and huge blue eyes. I'd had zero experience with kids, but Sylvia had plopped her infant onto my lap without preamble the very first day I'd come over to their tiny apartment.

"Watch her while I make lunch. Don't worry, she doesn't
bite." Then Sylvia grinned, twin dimples appearing in her
cheeks. "Well, she does, but she doesn't have teeth yet, so
you're safe."

I'd sat, petrified, my arms two iron bands around the
child, until she squirmed and squeaked in protest. But
it wasn't until Becca had given me an enormous, open-
mouthed smile and reached up to pat my cheek with her tiny
hand that I'd fallen completely in love.

And when Oliver made his appearance a few years later,
I'd been in the hospital, sitting in the waiting room until Linc
came bursting out, flushed and sweating, to tell me that he
had a son.

So while I understood that Sylvia's parents had done
the right thing, taking responsibility for their only daughter's children after her death had left Lincoln distraught and
all-too-frequently drunk, I couldn't stand the idea of Becca
and Oliver crying when their father had to leave. It made me
unreasonably angry.

"Listen, I don't want to talk about this anymore. Nothing I can do right now. Maybe next summer, after school's
out, I can take them with me for a little while. Anyway, I'll
be on-site by lunch time most likely. I'm in Tennessee right
now, and I'll probably make it to Georgia tonight, but I'm
going to wimp out and grab a motel room to get some sleep."

"That's not wimping out, dude, that's common sense.
I'd rather have you here a little later than lying in a ditch
along the highway." As soon as I spoken the words, I realized what I'd said and wished I'd bitten my tongue instead.

Shit. Not cool to talk like that when it'd been a terrible car accident that had taken Sylvia away from us all.

But if Linc noticed, he didn't show it. "Yeah, that's what I thought. Plus, if I get a decent night's sleep, I might be able to accomplish something tomorrow when I get there." I heard some background noise, a mechanical female voice which I recognized as the navigation system. "Okay, I'm just crossing into Georgia now. So how's it going with the lady boss?"

I frowned at the abrupt change in subject. "Uh, fine. You know, same old. We're coexisting, and I think we're mostly on the same page." The truth was, I hadn't seen Abby for more than a few minutes since the day I'd snapped at her about her dick of an ex. And each time we had been together, other people were around us. She'd gone back to being stiff and formal with me, and I treated her the way I would any virtual stranger.

"Uh huh. I'm not going to force you to tell me what's really going on until I get there. I'm too tired to tell you to get your ass in gear tonight. So maybe you should make nice with the lady and save me the trouble."

I clenched my jaw and counted to ten before answering. "Whatever you say, Linc. Drive safe, and I'll see you tomorrow."

"You know it." The click told me he'd hung up, and I grimaced as I slid the phone back into my pocket. Linc wasn't going to let me get away with giving Abby crap. He had strong feelings about our responsibility to the people who hired us, and he'd side with the owner every single time, unless it came down to the safety of our crew. I had the most annoying feeling that he and Abby would like each other once they met. Most likely they'd gang up against me. *Peachy.*

A low roll of thunder rumbled in the distance. I turned into the hallway, thinking to beat the rain and get back to my truck, when I heard the rustle of papers coming from the dining room. I frowned; all those windows should've been closed and locked, but it sounded like wind was blowing through the room. I muttered a curse under my breath and went back to double check.

The lists I could've sworn were rolled up in my pocket were scattered all over the gleaming floor. One blew across the room as I stepped in, and a chill slithered up my spine: all the windows were closed. There wasn't another source of moving air in here.

I bent slowly to collect the papers, tense and on alert. When I heard the sound of a closing door, my heart pounded nearly out of my chest. Fortunately, the noise was immediately followed by the click of heels, and I realized it had to be Abby. No one else wore those kind of shoes to the work site. She wasn't stupid; when she planned to be in the unfinished sections of the hotel, she conceded to sneakers, but otherwise, it was those prissy-girl shoes that made her legs look like they went on forever.

I reached for the last of the papers, but it slid just beyond my hand, almost as though someone had moved it away. I lost my balance and ended up sprawled on the floor. The heels came closer and stopped, their arrival punctuated by a sharp intake of breath.

"Oh, my God, Ryland, are you all right?"

I didn't move right away, partly because I was embarrassed that she'd found me on the floor and partly—okay, mostly—because I wanted to see what she'd do. I hadn't missed the fact that she'd slipped and called me by my first name again.

Abby knelt next to me, her knees against my ribcage and her hand touching my back. I lifted my head and pushed to sit up, but not before I caught the look in her eyes. It was alarm and worry, and the idea that Abby was worried about me gave me a feeling I didn't want to acknowledge.

"I'm fine." I rolled over and dropped to my ass. "I must've left these papers in here, and when I tried to pick them up, I, uh, slipped." I crumpled them in my fist. "What're you doing here, anyway?" My tone was sharper than I meant it to be.

She stood up, and I noticed her fingers rubbing together the fabric of her skirt, one of Abby's few nervous tells. Knowing I made her as jumpy as she did me somehow made me feel a little better.

"I didn't think anyone would be around, and I wanted to measure the windows in here. I forgot to do it this morning, and the interior designer needs the information right away."

"Why does she need to know about the windows? Cooper's taking care of that. He already has the measurements." I rose to my feet, too, and Abby took one step back.

"What does Coop have to do with the window dressings?" She put her hands on her hips, which I knew indicated she was ready for battle. *Great.*

"Window *dressings*? What the hell's that? Cooper's making exact replicas of the shutters that would've be on these doors originally. We found a picture, remember?"

"I remember." Abby pressed her lips together for a second, as though she was gathering her patience before going on. "I just don't remember how that picture translated into the idea of Cooper making shutters. And I'm also a little confused about why you think you have anything at all to do with the interior design of the hotel. Your job is structural restoration. If you were a plastic surgeon, doing reconstructive surgery, you wouldn't tell the woman you'd operated on what she could wear after you were done, would you? Same thing."

"I sure as hell wouldn't let her go around looking like a slut, with stupid curtains where there should be classic shutters."

She rolled her eyes. "That whole analogy just broke down. The point is that you have no say in what goes into or onto the hotel once you've finished the rebuild. And the curtains I'm ordering are not going to look slutty, whatever that means in interior design." She had that note in her voice, that almost bored, condescending I'm-the-expert-and-I'm-in-charge tone that made me want to punch one of our newly-finished walls.

"Look here, *princess*." I heard the nasty in my tone, but I was way beyond caring. "I get that you think you're running the show, that you're the big, bad hotel heiress. But I'm telling you, I'm not letting you screw up this hotel. I'm not letting something that could be beautiful and timeless morph into some cookie-cutter boutique place. It's not going to happen."

"Listen to me, *mister*." Her eyes flashed, her translucent

cheeks flushed and her full lips moved with intensity. She should've been pissing me the hell off. But for some reason known to no man, something surged inside me. The feeling was close to anger, but at the same time, it was different. Powerful and hard and undeniable—it was desire. I was arguing with Abby, about ready to wring her neck, and yet all I really wanted to do was grab her by those slim shoulders, yank her closer to me and kiss her until she shut up.

Shit.

I stood there, staring at her, unmoving, while she yammered on. I don't know what expression was on my face, but after a few minutes, she stopped talking. Her eyes narrowed, her forehead crinkled and she frowned.

"What's the matter with you? Are you having a stroke or a seizure or something? You look weird." She took a step closer. "Did you hit your head when you fell?"

"No." The word came out in almost a whisper. "No head trauma."

I watched, fascinated, as her face relaxed, her forehead smoothing out, eyes widening and softening. Her lips parted just enough for her tongue to creep out as the tip of it passed between. The sight snapped my thin band of control, and my hands reached forward, almost of their own accord.

I gripped her upper arms gently, my fingers rubbing the soft skin until she shivered. A soft breeze that came from God only knew where skimmed over us both, and suddenly I *wanted*. I wanted this woman so badly that I couldn't take my next breath unless my mouth was on hers. Without thinking about it, operating on pure driven instinct, I lowered my head, at the same time as I drew her body closer to mine.

I was nearly touching her lips when she jerked back, twisting out of my hands.

"No."

The single word slammed into me like a two-ton truck, knocking the wind out of my lungs. Abby hugged her arms around her middle and dropped her head, staring at the floor. Her back was moving up and down fast, and that gave it away: she'd been feeling it, too. Whatever this was between us, it wasn't one-sided. But she'd pushed me away anyway.

"Why?" I managed to croak the question.

"It's a bad idea, Ryland. A bad, bad idea. Getting involved with someone you work with is never good. And you—I—you hate me. You can't stand me."

"That's not true." My tongue was thick in my mouth. "I don't hate you. And when you relax, Donavan, you're very easy to like."

"But we argue all the time." She still wasn't looking at me. "And I'm older than you."

"Are you? Who the hell cares? What do a few years mean? And did you ever think that maybe we argue because we're both passionate?"

"I don't care. I can't. I can't do this."

A bolt of lightening split the dark sky, and for that moment I saw Abby's face clearly. Pain and panic were etched there, and involuntarily I stumbled back. I couldn't push her, that much was apparent, but neither was I going to let her get away with stupid excuses. I'd never known this chick to back down from a challenge, not when it was tossed right in front of her.

"Are you scared, Donavan? Is that it?"

TAWDRA KANDLE

I expected a flair of temper or even a sneer. Instead, she lifted her gaze to mine and answered in a voice filled with anguish.

"Of course I am."

Before I could say anything else, she turned and sprinted from the room, her shoes clattering over the floor. I took off after her, only because the rain was coming down in sheets now, and the lightening was putting on a terrifying show. No way in hell she should've been outside.

But the door slammed behind her. I gripped the knob, but it stuck, refusing to turn. It'd never done this before; the whole doorknob mechanism was new, and there was no logical reason why it wasn't working. I gave one more hard jerk, and it finally gave way.

By then, of course, Abby was long gone. I assumed she'd parked in her regular spot by the river, and I hoped she'd made it back to the car. Going after her at this point would only upset her more, and I'd already done a bang-up job of that.

A gust of wind blew through the open door and across the foyer. At the same time, softer air swirled around me, carrying the scent of flowers, just as I'd smelled before. I couldn't tell if the touch was meant to be comforting or accusatory.

"I just got carried away. Bad idea, I get it. I won't try it again." I spoke aloud, as though someone could hear.

Something rippled over the hotel, a noise or a vibration. It reminded me of my mother's frustration when I was being pig-headed; it was as though whatever or whoever was here didn't want me to give up on Abby Donavan.

90

"You heard her. She's scared. She can't see past the fear." Even as I said it, I felt an odd kind of despondency.

From down the hall, a whispered sigh reached my ears *She will.*

chapter six

Abby

"WELL, LOOK WHAT THE CAT dragged in." Alex Nelson came around the counter from the kitchen and pulled me into a quick, tight hug. "For someone who threatened us with stalking, you've been making yourself pretty damn scarce, beautiful."

"I know. I'm sorry." I squeezed him back and kissed his bristly cheek. "The Riverside's been keeping me busy." I let go of Alex and pulled out one of the chintz-covered bar-stools. "Plus, I figured it was a good idea to give you guys some space, let you find your own way here for a while. How's it going?"

Alex leaned his elbows on the countertop and grinned at me. "It's been amazing. You know, when Jude offered this to Cal and me, I thought to myself, *how clichéd is this?* I mean, the gay couple running a B&B. Seriously. And then Cal said to me, 'Who're we kidding? Cliché or no, it's living the dream.' And he was right. This is exactly what I've always wanted to do. And we're together, in the same city—hell, in the same damn *house*—so you won't hear this boy complaining. Not for real, anyway."

"Tell the truth, babe. You're in hog heaven." Cal came down the steps, carrying a basket of sheets. "Hey, Abby. How're you doing?"

"Can't complain." I smiled at him. I didn't know Cal as well as I did Alex, even though I'd met them at almost the same time. Alex was one of those people who was an instant friend; he was gregarious, outgoing and engaging. Cal took a little longer to warm up. Once I'd gotten past his guarded exterior, though, I'd understood why Alex had fallen head over heels for the art dealer from Savannah. Of course, the fact that Cal was tall and built, with dark hair and huge brown eyes that seemed fathoms deep, didn't hurt either. Next to Alex's sunny blondness, they looked like an ad for a high-class men's fashion magazine.

"I went by the Riverside last week. Looks like she's moving along well. Do you have an opening date set yet?" Alex poured each of us a tumbler of sparkling water and added a twist of lime.

"Tentative, but not announced. We're not close enough to put the final date in stone. The finishing crew arrives Monday, and once they get down to business, we should be able to gauge things better."

"Sounds good." Cal lifted up his basket and jerked his

head toward the back of the house. "If you'll excuse me a minute, I need to get these sheets in. Be right back."

I noticed that Alex's eyes followed his boyfriend as he navigated the tables and disappeared down the hall. Nudging him on the arm, I smirked. "So I guess it's safe to say all is well in paradise?"

He sighed, his lips curling. "You could say that. Hell, Ab, I'm happier than I've ever been. I never thought this could happen for me, but here I am, all domesticated and shit. Part of me keeps waiting for Cal to get spooked and disappear, but he seems . . . contented. I think he loves the Cove."

"What's not to love?" I sipped my water. "Beautiful beaches, friendly people, and warm weather."

"You're starting to sound like a local, kiddo. Are you settling down?"

I lifted one shoulder. "If I can manage it, yes. That's why I'm so excited about the Riverside. It'll let me stay in town and still work at an upscale hotel. There's room for growth, if Jude and Logan decide to expand the branding at all. Plus, it feels like home. I can't wait to move in and make it mine."

"Uh huh." Alex fixed me with a teasing smile. "And how are things going with the hunky contractor? You two still bickering?"

My face heated before I could help it, and Alex pushed against the tiled counter to stand up. "Ah, what's *this*? Are you blushing, Abigail Donavan? And just what is it—or who is it—making your cheeks go all rosy and your eyes shine?"

"Shut up, they're not." I pressed my palms against the

warm skin of my face. "It's just hot in here."

"Not really. But I'd say someone's definitely hot. Is it you, Ab? Are you lusting after the luscious Ryland?"

I dropped my forehead against the heel of my hand. "No. He's just—no. We fight constantly. I thought he hated me, but then last night, he—" I shook my head. "I don't know what happened."

"Oh, no, cupcake. You can't leave it at that. You gotta share the details."

"Alex, leave her alone." Cal came back into the room. He patted my back as he passed. "If Abby wants to tell us why you mentioning the, uh, restoration specialist with the killer six-pack makes her blush like a tomato, she'll do it in her own time." He shot me a wide and sunny smile.

"And just how do you know Ryland has a killer six-pack?" Alex quirked an eyebrow, but the twinkle in his eye told me he was teasing.

"Hey, I've got eyes. I might've seen him working around Cooper's place without his shirt on." He snaked an arm around Alex's shoulder. "I love you, but I'm not dead."

"You know, maybe Ryland's gay. I mean, damn. I love you, too, baby, but that dude's easy on the eyes."

"He's not gay." I spoke more definitively than I meant without thinking about it.

"Aha!" Alex pounced on my words like a cat on a mouse. "How do you know?"

"I . . ." Scrambling for an excuse, I tripped over my own tongue. "I just don't get that feeling, you know?"

"Oh, really? So did you not get that feeling when his tongue was down your throat, or is it just a hunch?"

My mouth fell open. "His tongue was *not*—no one's tongue has been anywhere. On me, I mean."

"But something did happen." Alex leaned toward me. "You're trying not to tell us something. I can see it in your eyes."

"It's nothing. And I don't want to talk about it." I pushed my glass away and crossed my arms.

"Hmmm. Something's inconsistent here. Either it's nothing, which means . . . well, nothing. Or you don't want to talk about it, which means it's something. Because you can't not want to talk about nothing."

"You lost me several nothings ago." I stood up. "And if you're going to harass me, I'm leaving. I can go hang out at Matt's store without anyone giving me a hard time."

"Abby!" Cal snagged my arm. "We're sorry. We were just teasing you." He glared at his partner. "Some of us tend to get carried away."

Alex had the good grace to look contrite. "Sorry, Ab. I really was just playing. I'm used to harassing Ali and Meghan. I only mess with the people I love, if it makes you feel any better."

I leaned the backs of my legs against the stool, not sitting back down but not stalking out yet, either. "I've never had anyone tease me like that." I glanced from Cal to Alex. "I didn't have brothers, and I never even really had that many friends growing up. My sister—well, we weren't close. So I guess I was overreacting a little."

Cal wrapped me in a big hug. "Don't sweat it. Just know that Alex and I are here to be your big brothers now. That might mean we annoy you sometimes, but we also have your

back all the time. And no one else better give you any shit."
His dark brows drew together, and I couldn't help giggling.
Cal might've been able to pull off intimidating with other
people, but I knew he was a teddy bear.

"Okay, enough of the schmaltz." Alex bumped his hip
against mine. "Seriously, now. Ryland's not being a problem, is he? I thought you two had worked out your issues."

I slumped against the chair. "I thought so, too. Then we
got into a spat a few weeks back, and ever since things have
been tense again."

"What did you fight over?" Cal crossed into the kitchen
and picked an apple out of the basket.

"Oh." I shifted my weight from one foot to the other.
"My ex-boyfriend."

Alex made a small strangled noise. "You fought over
your ex?"

I kicked myself mentally. This was opening up a whole
new can of worms. "Yes. My ex-boyfriend . . . he screwed
up my last job, up in Boston. I told Ryland about it, and then
he found out Zachary had applied to run the restaurant down
here at the Riverside."

"Oh, hell no." Alex put his hands on hips, frowning.
"You're not hiring him, are you?"

"God, how stupid do you all think I am? Of course not."
I paused. "But Ryland got pissy because I said I wasn't going
to throw away Zachary's resumé. I was just curious about
why he'd be interested in this job, when he actually ended up
with a pretty sweet gig after he ruined my career."

"Did you ever figure it out?" Alex sounded like Ryland—angry that I'd even care about the whys.

"Not really. I made some calls and found out he's still working for the same hotel I'd heard about. My contacts said they thought he'd been lying low since he left Boston. So I still don't have any idea why he'd want to trade that in for the job here."

Cal nodded. "I understand why you're wary about his motives, but I think I have to agree with the contractor and my guy here. Better to leave it alone." He paused a beat. "But Ryland was mad that you might see your ex. Hmm. The plot thickens."

"There's no plot." I tried to be both emphatic and casual at the same time, but I only came off sounding wishy-washy.

"Has he said anything to you about—what's his name? Zachary? I mean, since you fought."

"No." I kept my gaze on the floor. "Not about that."

"But about something else."

"Yes. No. Well . . . not really." I heaved a deep sigh. "Last night I went to the hotel, and Ryland was there. We got into a fight about the curtains in the dining room, and then the next thing I knew, he almost, um, kissed me. I think."

"Almost? As in, he didn't actually do it?" Alex was struggling to hold back a huge smile, I could tell.

"No, I pushed him away." I flushed again. "God, this is so embarrassing. Can we please stop talking about this? It's nothing. It means nothing. He was probably just messing around. Or maybe I misunderstood what was happening."

"You're probably right." Cal hooked his thumbs in the belt loops of his jeans. "He just tripped and landed on your lips. Happens all the time."

"No, I mean, it was just the heat of the moment. We

were arguing and he got carried away."

"Oh, sure." This time Alex was playing the role of smartass. "Same thing went down here last week. I was arguing with one of the workmen and next thing I knew, I was kissing him." He wagged his head in mock resignation. "So awkward."

"You know what, you're the ones who wanted to hear about what happened between Ryland and me. That's it. Now you know. And I promise there won't be any more to know, so you better make these little tidbits last." I hiked the strap of my purse more securely onto my shoulder. "Now I really am going over to Matt's. He won't coerce me into telling him secrets and then make fun of me."

"Aww, sweetie." Alex took my hand in his and lifted our joined fingers to his lips, kissing my knuckles. "We weren't making fun. It's just that you're so serious sometimes. We were trying to get you to lighten up."

I snorted. "Better men than you have taken on that mission, my friends. Being serious is who I am." I fingered the edge of the placemat that protected the table next to me. "And I haven't had much experience when it comes to men and romance. I had a few casual boyfriends in college, and then Zachary. I trusted him. I 'lightened up', like you said, and I shared secrets and laughed more and just wasn't so intense. And that really didn't turn out well at all. So the idea of going down that path again is terrifying."

Alex used the hand he held to draw me closer to him, and Cal flanked my other side, the two of them closing ranks around me in a way I knew was as figurative as it was literal.

"Abby, we love you just the way you are." Alex's voice

was muffled against my hair. "We don't want you to change."

"Not a bit." Cal kissed my cheek. "Some day I'll tell you my own story. I had a Zachary in my past, too—only his name was Rich. When I met this guy here, the last thing I wanted was to put myself at risk again. And serious?" He rolled his eyes. "I could've out-intensed you any day of the week. I thought Alex was some flighty dude, someone too much fun for a stick-in-the-mud like me."

A rush of understanding filled me. I related to this. "So what happened?"

Cal laid a hand on Alex's shoulder and squeezed. "He didn't give up. He kept coming around. He didn't push too hard, but he didn't let me keep pulling back, either. He called me on my shit when I was treating him the way I thought I had to in order to protect myself. He reminded me he wasn't Rich, and eventually I figured out I could trust him."

I chewed the side of my lip. "That's sweet, Cal. And you two are perfect for each other." I gave each of them a little extra hug. "But it's not the same with Ryland. He's not trying to win me over. If he really is interested in something with me, it's only temporary. Nothing long-term. I'm not sure I can handle a fling."

I didn't miss the glance the guys exchanged over my head. "Maybe a fling is exactly what you need, though, Abby. You know, just a little mindless . . . fun." Alex smoothed his hand over my hair.

"I don't think I'm made that way. I've never had . . . you know . . . without some kind of commitment. Or at least deep feelings."

"But you never know." This time Cal smiled down

100

at me. "Some of the best couples start out casual. Look at Meghan and Sam."

"And Emmy and Cooper," Alex added. "You just never know what might happen if you give it a chance. Open yourself up—just a little."

I drew in a deep breath. "I'll take it under consideration. But now I really do have to go." I glanced around the kitchen, a room that used to be as familiar to me as my own face in the mirror. Now I could see subtle differences, changes Alex and Cal had added to make it their own. It wasn't mine anymore. While that gave me a small pang of sadness, I knew it was how things were supposed to be.

"You guys have done a great job here. I knew my baby was in good hands, and now I'm happy that you've made her yours." I stood on tiptoe to kiss first Alex's cheek and then Cal's. "Well done."

"Change isn't always easy, but it happens." Alex arched a brow at me, and I knew he was talking about more than the Hawthorne House. "We have two choices: we can fight it, which never works, or we can roll with it, which is scary. Either way, you're going to end up in a different place than where we started. It's just a matter of which path you choose to get there, the rocky one or the smooth one."

"Thank you, oh wise one." I skirted a chair and pushed open the door. "I'm taking all this advice down to the Tide for a drink. See you later."

Humid salt air hit me as I rounded the corner of the B&B and headed for the main street of town. The afternoon was waning, and the sun was low in the sky. As much as I loved living in the Cove, and in Florida in general, I still missed autumn in the northeast, with the changing leaves and cooler temps. Down here, the only change was a little respite from intense heat and slightly shorter days. Oh, and of course the change in crowds. During the summer months, the beaches were filled with families, with parents on vacation and children on school breaks. This time of year, we were just beginning to see the snow birds whose numbers would swell after Christmas. Fall tended to be a quieter time when it came to tourists, and while I knew they were a huge part of our business, I liked having our little town mostly to ourselves.

"Whoa there." Strong hands caught my shoulders. "Almost ran me over there, Abby."

I smiled up at Matt Spencer and stepped to the side of the sidewalk. "Sorry about that. I guess I was zoning out. I was actually just going to see if you were still at the store. I wanted to talk with you about the space for the surfboard rental kiosk at the Riverside."

"I'm about to head home." Matt beamed. "Sandra's still recovering, and I don't like to leave her with all the baby work if I can help it."

I laughed. "You mean you hate to be away from that adorable little girl any longer than you have to be." Matt and Sandra's baby Gillian was only a few weeks old, and Matt, a first-time dad, was besotted with her.

"Pretty much." He grinned, not at all bothered by the admission. "What can I say? I've always been a sucker for a cute girl. Oh, hey, check this out. I took it this morning on my way out the door. Isn't she gorgeous?"

"This one's going to have you wrapped around her finger forever." I shaded my eyes against the rays of the setting sun as I looked at the picture on his phone. "I'm so happy for you, Matt. For both you and Sandra. How's Lily adjusting to the new family member?" Sandra had been a widow when she met Matt a few years ago; Lily was her daughter from her first marriage.

"Like a champ. She helps out so much, it's crazy. I couldn't be prouder of her." He leaned down toward me. "We haven't told anyone yet, but I'm going to adopt Lily. We started the process a few months back."

"Oh, that's wonderful." I thought that Matt just might burst with happiness. He was practically glowing. "Look at you, with this beautiful family. You truly are blessed."

"I am." His grin faded as his eyes grew serious. "I'll tell you, Abby, a few years ago, I never would've imagined this could happen to me. After Daniel passed away, I kind of fell into a slump. I figured my life was just about over, too. He was one of my best friends, and he was gone. I'd screwed up my own chance at marriage and family a long time ago. When the posse suggested that one of us should romance Jude, I figured, why not? At least I wouldn't be alone any-more." He hunched his shoulders over, dropping his voice. "If Jude hadn't decided to set me up with Sandra . . . well, what I have with her is beyond anything I could've imag-ined. It's more than companionship. I really did find the love of my life. And now I have two little girls, too."

A lump rose in my throat. "That's so beautiful, Matt. Sandra's a lucky woman."

He shook his head. "Nah, it's me who got the better end of this deal. Far more than I deserve, believe me." He glanced down at his phone again, checking the display. "Hey, I hate to do this, but can we talk about the kiosk on Monday? I'll stop by your office at lunch time, if it's okay. I really need to get home."

"Of course." I stepped back. "Give Sandra my best. And if there's anything you all need, let me know. Happy to help."

"Thanks, Abby. See you later." Matt jogged back across the street, practically sprinting toward where I assumed his car was parked behind the surf shop. I stifled a sigh, feeling suddenly alone. Although I knew it wasn't true, today it felt like the whole world was matched up. Everyone I knew was happy and in love, while I was heading back to my lonely and silent apartment above the Tide.

Oh, scratch the silent. I'd forgotten it was Saturday night, which meant a live band playing at the bar. *Terrific.*

I had a hot date with my headphones. And if things really got wild, I might even run a hot bath and soak in some bubbles.

With a heaviness I couldn't shake, I made my way toward the Riptide and another empty evening.

chapter seven

Ryland

" **I** HAVE TO SAY, I'M IMPRESSED." Linc stood with me on the porch of the Riverside, looking up. "Once again, you saw the potential where I only saw problems. Good job, man."

No matter how many times this scene played out, I always felt a tickle of pride when Linc affirmed my work. Or at least my intuition, in this case. I had a father and a grandfather, and they were both supportive and encouraging. But Linc knew the job. He understood it—and me—in a way no one else did. When he told me I'd gotten one right, it felt good.

"I told you she's a beauty." I leaned against the railing of the porch. "All we've got to do is finish her up. Add some polish, a few details. Make sure it's all pretty. And done the right way."

"Ah." Linc swiped the cap off his head and shot me a look, eyes narrowing. "You're still fighting the lady boss, aren't you? Dammit, Ry, we've talked about this. *They* hire us. We do what the client wants. We can advise and we can inform, but we don't make the final call."

"Even when they're screwing shit up?" I scowled.

"Even when. And even if the lady boss is an ice queen, a frigid bitch. We play nice, or we end up with a reputation for being hard to work with, and jobs dry up. In this economy, we can't afford to have too much in the way of principles about historic accuracy, dude. Someday, maybe. After you make the cover of *Historic Homes Restored* or whatever. You know that's how it is."

"I might know it, but I don't have to like it." I rubbed my jaw. "And she's not. Not really."

Linc's forehead wrinkled. "What? Who isn't?"

"Abby. She's not an ice queen. She's just—this place is important to her, too. Not for the same reasons as me, but it is. She comes off cold, but she's good at her job, and sometimes she's even right about it. Even if I hate it."

The lines on Linc's face smoothed out, and he nodded slowly, regarding me. "Okay. I see. I get it."

"You get what?"

"You. And the lady boss. You're sweet on her."

The words hit me way too close to the truth, and instinctively, I kicked back. "No, I'm not."

"Yeah, you are. You like her. You want her."

"Dude, no way. She makes me crazy."

Lincoln's short bark of laughter only made me pissi-
er. "Not like that. She makes me want to punch something.
She's prickly and smug and a know-it-all. Not my type."

"And yet . . ." Linc spread his hands in front of him.
"Your eyes do something funny when you talk about her."

"Yeah, they twitch, because she annoys the hell out of
me. Wait'll you meet her, you'll see."

"Uh huh. She coming to the site this afternoon?"

I shook my head. "I doubt it. She was here late yesterday." The image of her face before she'd turned tail and run
flashed through my brain.

"Oh, boy. What'd you do?" Linc stood with his hands
on his hips, staring me down.

"What do you mean? I didn't do anything."

"Bullshit. You've got a guilty look on your face."

I ran one hand over my eyes. "We got into it. Things got
. . . intense."

"And?"

"Isn't that enough? Does there have to an and?"

"Doesn't have to be, but there is. Did you lose your temper?"

"Yeah, at first." I looked away, out toward where I knew
the river was, beyond the trees. "And then I kind of tried to
kiss her."

For a solid minute, Linc stood there, not speaking. And
then he began to laugh. "Boy, you are so sunk."

I clenched my jaw. "It was stupid. Heat of the moment
crap. We were yelling at each other, and then . . .I don't know.
I grabbed her and I was about two seconds away from pushing her up against the wall and—well, I don't know what

would've happened next."

"But the lady said no?"

A tic jumped in my cheek. "Yeah. Well, she pushed me away. Left in a big hurry."

"And you haven't seen her since?" Lincoln shifted to sit down on the porch step, twisting so he could still see me.

"Nope. It was only last night. She doesn't always come to the site, not every day." I was quibbling, and I knew it. Abby came by this hotel at least once every day; if it wasn't first thing, on her way to the office, it was only because we had arrangements to meet at another point in the day, to deal with permits or talk to a work team. I'd spent this morning getting the main building ready for our details crew, lingering there longer than I needed to, on the off-chance Abby might stick to her routine and stop by.

But of course, she hadn't. I'd spooked her last night, and now everything was going to be even more awkward between us. She'd put up higher walls, freeze me out even more, and maybe even avoid being alone with me altogether. I wasn't sure whether or not to tell myself it was better this way or to curse the impulsiveness that had made me try for the kiss.

"You're going to have to make it right, Ry. We can't have a problem with a client, not after all the time and work you've put into this. Go talk to her, make nice, apologize, grovel, whatever the hell you need to do. Then we get through the rest of this restoration, get a glowing recommendation and head for the next job. Got it?"

I jerked my head. "Sure, whatever. But you don't know Abby. She's not going to like it if I try to apologize. She'd rather have us just forget it ever happened. Sweep it under the rug. That's just how she is."

Linc shrugged. "If you're sure about that, then fine. Do it your way. Only make sure she's not upset." He paused, considering. "What about her bosses? Will she tell them about what you did? Complain? We don't need any sexual harassment charges coming down at us."

"No way." I shook my head vehemently. "That's not how Abby operates. She takes care of her own problems. Last thing she'd do is go crying to Jude and Logan, because she'd be afraid doing that would make her look weak. I'm telling you, Linc, she's made of steel."

"Okay, good. Make sure things are cool with her, then, and let's keep moving." He stood up and turned in a slow circle to take in the rest of the property. "So we'll get the guys in here to start the finishing work, while the local crew completes the outbuildings. Once they're done, we'll move over there and get going. I figure . . ." He squinted, lips pressed tight as he ran it through in his head. "Six weeks. Eight at tops, if the weather interferes. Of course, we'll be mostly inside from here on out." He glanced at me. "Have you set up with the landscapers?"

I lifted one shoulder. "Abby took care of that. We're all supposed to meet next week, I think."

"Good. We'll get down to business, then." Linc stretched, groaning as his back arched. "Did you get me a room at the motel in town?"

"Nope. I've got an extra bedroom over at Cooper's place, so I figured you could bunk with me. Nicer than having to deal with the guys."

"Yeah, I guess. Think they'll be okay without supervision?"

I laughed. "They're all adults, Linc. And what're you going to do, follow them around and babysit? They might get into trouble, but no more than if you were sitting in a cramped little motel room. It's not like you're going to tuck them in every night or have a curfew. And Coop's house is really comfortable."

"Sounds like a plan." One side of his mouth quirked up. "As long as I won't be, ah, cramping your style. You know, if you and the lady boss decide to mix it up after all. I don't need to hear all the moans and squeaky bed springs."

I shot him a one-fingered salute. "Not going to happen. Your virgin ears will be safe, I promise." I pushed off the porch railing and jogged down the steps. "You're right. The last thing I need to be doing is messing around with a client. From here on out, it's all business."

Linc punched me on the arm. "Thanks, Ry. I know I'm a hard ass about that stuff. And I know I don't really have the right to tell you what to do, seeing that I'm not a partner. But I couldn't be more invested if I were." He cleared his throat. "Now how about taking me into town for a drink? It's been a long day."

I glanced at him, worrying snaking around my heart. "A drink?"

He grinned and rolled his eyes. "Yeah, a ginger ale on the rocks. That's all I want. We'll get you a beer, we'll chat it up with the locals and then I'm hitting the hay. And you, my friend, can fill me in on everything else that's been going on here." He clapped his hand on my back. "It's good to be back with you, man."

The Riptide was already busy by the time Linc and I stepped up to the bar. I found us two stools, and we sat down as Emmy waved to me from the other end.

"Hey, Ryland." She smiled as she approached us. "How're you doing tonight?"

"Can't complain, Emmy. This is Lincoln Turner. He's my unofficial business partner—meaning he does everything a partner would, but he doesn't want the title. He'll be in town for the rest of the Riverside job."

Emmy wiped her hand on the bar rag and extended it to Linc. "Nice to meet you. I'm Emmy Carter, and I run the Tide on weekend nights."

"And her boyfriend Cooper owns the house where I've been staying." I glanced at the pretty redhead. "Linc's taking the second bedroom at Coop's house. I cleared it with Cooper first."

She waved her hand. "Hey, the more, the merrier as far as I'm concerned. Cooper's just happy someone's living in the house." She leaned one hip against the bar. "Now what can I get you gentlemen?"

"Is it too late to get a burger?" I looked over her shoulder into the kitchen. Dinner service ended before the music began, and only bar food was served thereafter.

"Nah, grill's still open. What'll it be?"

"How about a Ripper burger for each of us, medium

well, a side of fries, a beer for me and a ginger ale for my buddy here?"

Emmy rapped her knuckles on the oak bar. "Coming right up." She pulled down two mugs. "I hope you're planning to hang around for the band tonight. They're from Tampa, and it's their second time here. I think they're going to be huge."

I glanced at Linc. "Up to you, buddy. I know you've had a long day of driving to get here."

"Let's see how I feel after eating."

Emmy set our drinks in front of us. "So, Lincoln, is it? Seems like you're a little late to the game, huh? Isn't the hotel nearly finished?" She glanced my way. "At least that's what Abby tells me."

Linc nodded. "Seems that way, doesn't it? Actually, I head up the details crew. We come in after Ryland and the local workers have done all the hard stuff, and we make it look pretty." He winked at her. "And call me Linc."

"Don't let him fool you. The finishing touches are some of the most important in this job." I took a long drink of my beer. "It's an artisan job. Linc'll be working closely with Cooper, so I'm anxious for them to meet."

Emmy's eyes brightened, and her smile grew soft. "Oh, he'll love that. He's got such a gift, you know? Just takes my breath away."

I nudged my friend. "Not that she's biased or anything."

"Not a bit. I actually fell in love with Cooper's work a long time before I gave the man himself the time of day." She turned toward the kitchen. "Hey, Aaron, two Rippers and a new basket of fries, okay?"

THE PATH

The bar slowly filled as Linc and I enjoyed our hamburgers. He fancied himself a connoisseur of burgers, so I wasn't surprised when he raved over the buffalo-sauce and blue cheese sandwich.

The band was just beginning to warm up when Emmy returned to check on us. She refilled Linc's ginger ale and offered me a second beer. I hesitated, but Linc pushed the empty mug toward her.

"Go ahead, give him another." He stood up and grabbed his baseball cap. "I think I'm going to walk back to the house. It's a beautiful night, and I could use the exercise after being stuck in the car for two days."

I swiveled around on my stool. "You sure? I'll drive you back. I don't need to stay here."

Linc shook his head. "Nah. You're young. Stay, have another drink, flirt with the pretty girls." He jerked his chin in the direction of the cluster of women beginning to crowd the small stage. "That blonde chick in the shorts and jean jacket's been eyeing you up all night. Have some fun, man." A small, sad smile played over his lips. "Have some fun for me."

I watched him make his way through the throngs of people standing between the tables until he disappeared through the door. When I turned back, Emmy wore an inscrutable expression.

"He's got a story, doesn't he?"

I gave a little shrug. "Don't we all?"

"True enough, my friend. Okay. Let me set you up with another beer, then I'm going to make sure the band has everything they need." She cast her eyes upward toward the ceiling. "I love our live music Saturdays, but now that Abby's living upstairs, I feel bad about how loud it is. She says it isn't a problem, but I bet some nights the pictures on her wall are rattling."

"She's up there now?" I hadn't thought about Abby living above the bar. Her personality was so utterly opposite of the casual, laid-back atmosphere at the Tide that it seemed impossible for the two to coexist.

"Yeah, she came in just a little while before you did. Usually she hangs out down here for a while before she goes up, but tonight she didn't even stop to talk. Just gave me a wave and ran upstairs." Emmy narrowed her eyes at me. "Everything okay at the hotel? You didn't give her a hard time, did you?"

I clapped my hand over my heart. "Why do you assume it was *me* giving *her* a hard time? Maybe she was busting my balls. Ever think about that?"

Emmy cocked her head at me and raised one eyebrow. "Ryland, I like you. But Abby's my best friend, and I know her. She seems tough, but that's just her exterior. You'd be surprised how easily she can be hurt."

I thought about the expression in her eyes last night, and something inside me shriveled. "Yeah, maybe. But to answer your question, I didn't even see her today." Which was true, even though I knew what was bothering Abby probably had more to do with last night than with anything that had happened since.

"Hmmm. Well, maybe she was just tired. She works damn hard, that one."

I smirked. "Isn't that the pot calling the kettle black?"

Emmy laughed. "Touché. Although I've slowed down quite a bit since Cooper's moved in with me. I have a lot more fun these days." She untied her apron and rounded the end of the bar. "Speaking of which, it's time to start us up. I'll be back to check on you in a few."

My eyes followed Em as she headed toward the guys on the stage. The blonde girl whom Linc had pointed out to me earlier smiled at me when my gaze traveled that way. She was pretty in a non-memorable way, which was generally how I liked my women. Nothing to make me stick, nothing to hold me down. Just innocent, harmless fun, over in one night and as quickly forgotten as the beer I'd just drained. A woman like that was just who I needed tonight; a little flirting, a little making out in the shadows. I thought of my truck parked in the Tide's lot. Maybe a little more than that, if she was willing. Anything to drive thoughts of Abby Donavan from my head.

The lights dimmed, and a single spotlight focused on Emmy standing on the stage in front of the band.

"Hello, Crystal Cove! Welcome to Saturday night at the Riptide. Tonight, we're excited to welcome back Tampa's very own rising stars, The Bay Runners!"

Cheers and shouts rose as the guitar began to sing, soon joined by the voice of the kid playing it. I smothered a sigh; when I had I started thinking of anyone under the age of twenty-five as a kid?

"Hi there." A soft hand touched my arm, and I wasn't at all surprised when I glanced down and realized that the hand belonged to Blondie. She gave me a tentative smile that matched the hesitation of her whispery voice.

"Hey." I forced a return grin.

"Great band, aren't they?" She moved closer to be heard, and in the process pushed her breasts against my side. "I saw them here in February. I just had to come back tonight."

"Yeah." I reached for my beer and tipped it against my mouth.

"Were you here that night? It was wild! All the spring break kids were going crazy." She giggled. "Someone spilled a whole pitcher of beer on me, and I was wearing a white T-shirt. It was so embarrassing!"

The way she said it told me that she hadn't been embarrassed at all. I gave myself permission to imagine her in a see-through shirt and waited for my body's reaction. Yeah, there it was. I was still alive and well. I let my gaze drift down her body and took in the boobs currently smushed against me. They were nice, I decided. More than nice. She had a generous rack, and I liked that in a woman. Right?

"No, I wasn't here that night. I'm not from the Cove. I'm just in town for a little while on a job." I finished my beer and pushed the empty mug across the bar.

"I'm Lacie." She had to practically shout for me to hear her now, even though she was almost climbing my body.

"Ryland." I turned my mouth to her ear, and as I spoke, someone jostled us, tipping Lacie off-balance. I caught her by the hips and let my hands rest there, just above her ass.

A smile curved her lips, and she wriggled against me. I felt her hardened nipples against my arm, through the thin tank top she was wearing. Nope, no bra there. Right about now, I should be hauling this chick up so that I could kiss her. It was dark over here, and everyone's attention was focused on the band. I could kiss her, feel her up . . . and then see where things went from there.

But damn it. I had zero desire to do that. Even when I pictured us in my truck, with Lacie straddling me while I palmed those luscious tits, my dick only gave me a half-hearted response. And even though I didn't want to admit it, I knew why. It was because of the woman a floor above us, who was probably already in bed, maybe with a pillow over her ears to muffle the noise of the bar. I smiled, picturing Abby trying to drown out the music. For some reason, I saw her in a long white nightgown like the ones women wore a century ago. That would suit her more than anything else, I decided.

Lacie brought my attention back to her when she slid one hand down my chest to rest between my legs. My body reacted, of course; I was a man and I was alive. A girl touches the cock, and it's going to spring to attention. That was just biology.

With the fingers that weren't currently in possession of my manhood, she gripped my wrist and bought my hand to her boob. Leaning into me, she bit my earlobe and whispered, "I live in an apartment around the corner, and my roommates are going to be gone all night. Want to get away from the crowd?"

There it was: my golden opportunity to get laid, gift-wrapped and handed to me on a silver platter. If I believed in shit like fate and destiny, I'd have lit out of that bar with Loosey Lacie over my shoulder, taken her to her empty apartment and banged the hell out of her until sunlight.

Instead, before I could even stop and think about it, I

backed away. I pulled my hand off her tit and her hand off my dick. Holding both her wrists in my fingers, I smiled and tried to let her down gently.

"Lacie, you're very pretty, and I'm sure you're a nice girl. But I'm not really into one-night hookups." *Since when?* I ignored the voice in my head. "And since I'm just kind of passing through town, that's all tonight could be. So you should check out some of the local guys. I bet you'd have a better time. But thanks for the offer."

Her mouth turned down, and her eyes blazed. "Yeah? Well, fuck you, Ryan or whoever the hell you are. Any other guy in this bar would die to get the chance to go home with me." She kicked at my barstool and stormed off until she was absorbed by the crowd.

"Smart move there." Emmy was suddenly back, retrieving my empty mug as she winked at me. "That girl gets around. I'm impressed you turned her down. Most guys don't." She shook her head. "It's sad, really. I'd be devastated if my daughter acted like that."

"Yeah." It was all I could manage at the moment. Some part of my physiology was still incredulous that we'd told Lacie no.

"Want another beer? It's on the house, for being such a decent guy."

I thought about it for a moment. "No thanks on the beer—I have to drive home, and two's my limit when I'm behind the wheel—but how about a root beer and I'll say thanks?"

Emmy laughed. "You got it."

For the next two songs, I nursed my soda and brooded.

My mind kept returning to Abby. To the way her smile lit up her whole face when she actually let herself relax. To the sound of her voice when she was trying to convince me that her way was better. To the vulnerability in her eyes on the afternoon she'd told me about her douchebag of an ex-boyfriend, and to the stark terror there when I'd been about to kiss her.

I thought of the way her legs looked in those ridiculous heels, and the sassy sashay of her ass in the short skirts she sometimes wore. I remembered the glimpse of cleavage I'd gotten when she'd leaned to examine the wainscoting in the hall one day. What I'd seen wasn't the overabundance possessed by Lacie, but it'd gotten me hard anyway. And just remembering, I had to shift in my seat and adjust my pants.

Damn it all to hell. Abigail Donavan was the last person in the world I wanted to desire. I'd promised Linc. And she'd been right last night, too; it was bad business to get involved with someone I worked with. And we had nothing in common. Zero. Zilch. She was stiff, rigid, uncompromising. *Ice queen.* Except, as I'd said to Linc today, she really wasn't. That was just the defensive exterior she kept up. When the ice melted, I had a feeling Abby Donavan burned hot.

And I wanted that heat. I wanted it right now, as much as I'd wanted it last night when I'd pulled her against me.

Without giving myself a spare minute to second-guess my actions, I stood up and pushed my way through the crowd. The band was playing its last song before a break, so not one person paid any attention to me. When I reached the far side of the restaurant, I maneuvered through until I found the door that led up the steps to the second level.

I'd never been up there, of course. But I knew she was at the top of the stairs, and I didn't hesitate. I took the steps two at a time to the landing. Once I reached it, I knocked on the door.

Emmy was right; the music was loud up here, too. I wondered if Abby would even be able to hear me over it. I briefly considered waiting until this song ended, but waiting had lost its appeal as an option. I pounded on the door again.

Still nothing. In frustration, I gripped the doorknob, thinking maybe she'd hear the rattle if I shook it enough. But to my utter amazement, it turned in my hand, and the door swung open.

I had about the length of a breath to spy her across the room before she saw me. Abby was sitting on a worn sofa with headphones over her ears, which explained why she hadn't heard my knocking. She had a book in her hand, and her legs were curled under her. She wasn't wearing the long white cotton nightgown I'd envisioned; instead, she had on a pair of black yoga pants and a green T-shirt.

I stood frozen, still in shock that the door had been unlocked. Abby must have either sensed me or caught my movement out of the corner of her eye; surprise flooded her face, and then in a delayed reaction that might've been hilarious under other circumstances, she shrieked and scrambled up to the back of the sofa.

Once it filtered into her brain that it was me and not some random attacker standing in the doorway of her apartment, terror gave way to mad. She jumped to her feet, threw her book onto the sofa cushion and tore off the headphones.

"What the *hell* are you doing here?" She screamed the

words, and distractedly I thought I'd never seen Abby so out of control. I liked it. "Who do you think you are, just walking into someone's apartment?"

"I knocked." It sounded lame, especially in the face of her fury. I tried again. "I knocked and I pounded, and you couldn't hear me." I pointed to the headphones. "I guess because you had those on."

She hugged her arms around her middle. "So that's what you do? If you go to someone's house and they don't answer, you just burst right in? Who are you? Goldilocks?"

It took me a minute to follow what she meant, and then I had to bite back a laugh. Abby's quick wit was just another point in her favor. I closed the door behind me, slowly getting back my equilibrium and with it, the pulsing desire that had driven me up here to her.

"I wanted to see you." I took two steps into the tiny living room.

Abby glanced behind her, as though judging how much space she had for retreat. I moved closer, and she tightened her arms around her ribs, sucking in her bottom lip. "Did you think that maybe I don't want to see you?"

I stopped just in front of her, hooking my thumbs in the front pockets of my jeans. "I don't think that's true."

She raised one eyebrow, and I could tell she was trying to pull her armor back into place. Only the tremble of her fingers as they clutched at her arm hinted at her fear. "Are you calling me a liar?"

I laughed. "No, Abby, I don't think you're a liar." I reached out one finger to tuck a strand of black hair behind her ear. "And I don't think you're a coward either."

"Why are you here? Can't whatever this is wait until Monday?" She took a step back, but she couldn't go any further, and she raised wide green eyes to mine.

"No, it really can't." I lifted my hand slowly to her face, cupping her cheek. "I couldn't wait one more minute to do this."

Without giving her a chance to protest, I tilted her head back and covered her lips with mine. She didn't respond for several seconds; she stood still as a statue, her mouth unmoving. I had a moment of misgiving, wondering if I'd really read her so wrong. If I were the only who wanted this.

And then with strangled cry, her arms dropped from her own waist and slid around me. She moved her lips to match my kisses, and I groaned, opening my mouth and coaxing her to do the same. When her tongue darted out to stroke against mine, an explosion of want erupted inside me.

I kept one hand on her face and lowered the other to her hip, pressing her closer to me. Abby rose up on her toes, seeming as eager to consume me with her hot little mouth as I was to have her. I could've easily laid her out on the couch and taken her there and then, or shoved her up against the wall and pounded myself into her softness. God knew I wanted to do it, and I wasn't at all sure she'd stop me this time.

But some sane part of me knew that I had to take things slow with Abby. This—me kissing her, her kissing me back—was a big first step, and I could ruin that by demanding more. So instead I contented myself with memorizing her mouth, lazily trailing my tongue over hers, and letting my fingers gently caress her hip over the cotton of her T-shirt. I became aware of her gradually relaxing against me, her shoulders easing and her fingers loosening their tight grip on my back.

I drew away from her mouth slowly, dropping small kisses at each corner of her lips and then trailing down her jaw to the soft skin on the side of her neck. Swirling my tongue around her earlobe, I paused to whisper in her ear.

"Abby? I like kissing you."

I was prepared for her to pull away, push back and retreat again. But I wasn't ready for her quiet laugh, and it utterly disarmed me. My heart lurched, and that was the moment Abigail Donavan completely owned me.

"I like kissing you, too, Ryland."

I tempted fate by pulling back a little and looking into her eyes in pretend shock. "Aha! You do know my first name."

She smiled and shook her head, and a lovely shade of pink deepened on her cheeks. "Yes, I know your name, and you know I do." She reached her fingers to smooth back my hair from my face. "Not that I'm complaining, but what made you come up here tonight? Why this . . ." She pointed at herself and then at me. "Why now?"

I linked my hands behind her back and studied her pretty face. "I don't know why now. I mean . . ." I was always a proponent of brutal honesty, and if Abby were going to get mad about the girl groping me down in the bar, I'd rather she did it now, hearing it from me. "I was downstairs having dinner with Linc. After he left, I stayed to listen to the band, and some girl came over to me." Abby tensed a little, and I held her a bit closer. "She was kind of touchy-feely. And she invited me back to her apartment for the night." I leaned forward to kiss the top of Abby's head. "I could've gone. I don't owe anyone anything—or rather, at that minute I didn't. But I realized that I wasn't interested. I didn't want a random chick from a bar. Not when the only woman I wanted to kiss and hold was right upstairs." I kissed her lips this time, lightly and fast. "That's you, by the way."

"I figured that out." The old dry tone was back in Abby's voice, and I was glad. "But why me? We haven't gotten along from the minute we met. And what I said yesterday still holds. We work together. And I'm older than you." She narrowed her eyes. "You don't have a mother complex, do you?"

I couldn't help laughing. "No, sweetheart, no mother complex here. I have a perfectly fine mom, and our relationship is so healthy it's boring. You being older than me means nothing. It's a few years, right? I mean, Ab, how old are you, anyway?" I tickled her side until she bent, giggling. "You're not one of those Inca mummy girls who looks sixteen but is really a few thousand years old, are you? Because yeah, that'd be a deal breaker."

She shook her head. "I'm thirty-three. And I'm not ashamed of my age. I just . . . you're younger. I don't want to feel like some skeevy old woman robbing the cradle."

"Yeah, I'm twenty-eight. That's five years. Now, if you were twenty and I were fifteen, you might qualify for the skeevy. But you're not and I'm not. We're both adults. It doesn't matter to me. Why should it bother you?"

"But we do work together." She hadn't pulled away from me yet, and I was counting that as a good sign. "That might not be such a good idea."

"We work together on this project. I'm not going to be one of your employees at the hotel once it's done, and you won't be mine. That's a short-term issue, and I don't think it's one that even applies here." I slid my hands up to her ribs, just barely teasing the sides of her breasts but not going any further. "I promise you, Donavan, I won't use sex to get my way when we argue about decisions at the Riverside." I bowed my head and skimmed my lips up her neck until she shivered. "On the other hand, I wouldn't discourage you from doing the same."

Abby smiled a little and sighed, dropping her forehead against my chest. "Do you want to sit down? I can get you something to drink. I don't have much up here, just some water and a bottle of wine."

"I don't need anything." I sank down onto the sofa and tugged her to sit with me. "And I should probably get back to Cooper's since this is Linc's first night in town. I mean, he's most likely sound asleep already, but just in case."

"What did he think of the hotel?" Abby arranged herself alongside me, tucking her feet up beneath her again. I draped my arm over her shoulder so that she was pressed up next to my side.

"He was very impressed. Estimates about six to eight weeks before you can open, barring some weather-related emergency. He wants to be in on the landscaping meeting next week, if that's okay."

"Of course. I'm looking forward to meeting him." She burrowed her head down a little more against me. "Ryland? Just so you know . . . I'm still scared of this. Of us. I know it sounds stupid, but I need us to move real slow." She hesitated, and I ran my finger down the smooth skin of her arm in encouragement. "I jumped into everything with Zachary. And I know you're not him, and I know I'm smarter now. But still, I have to be careful, for my own mental well-being."

"I understand. You're right." I thought of Linc's warning to me earlier. "And maybe we need to be kind of discreet until the hotel project's wrapped up, so that we don't raise any eyebrows."

"Probably a good idea." She knit her hands together and fiddling with her fingers. "So after the hotel is finished, you'll be moving on to the next job?"

I knew where she was going with this, and I swallowed a sigh. The last thing I wanted to think about right now was leaving Abby, but it was way too soon to talk about any alternative. I lifted one shoulder in a half-shrug.

"I guess so. Nothing's booked right now. Winter tends to be our slow time, since no one wants to pay us when weather delays are fairly inevitable, even in the south." I twisted a lock of her hair around my finger. "Of course, maybe I could find something in south Florida. That's about the only part of the country guaranteed not to get snow."

"Except Hawaii." She sounded so serious, but I laughed anyway.

"Right, except Hawaii. Unfortunately, doing jobs over there is too cost-prohibitive for us. Getting our team across the ocean, bringing in materials . . . it's not in the cards. Not yet, anyway."

Abby didn't answer, and I rubbed her back. "Let's take everything one day at a time, okay? Like you said . . . slow."

I sat up a little, turning her to face me again. "But right now I'd better get over to Cooper's. Since the band's still rocking downstairs, I can slip out without anyone knowing I was up here." I tipped her chin up, using one finger, and slanted my mouth over hers, reveling in the soft yield of her lips, the easy way she opened to me and the feel of her fingers digging into my shoulders.

She walked me to the door, and although she tiptoed to kiss me once more, her face had shuttered again. I tried not to let it bother me; there was no doubt in my mind that opening Abby Donavan's heart was a work in progress.

But it would be worth it.

chapter eight

Abby

"THAT WAS ABSOLUTELY DELICIOUS." EMMY leaned back from the table and sighed, rubbing her flat stomach. "Why didn't we do this sooner?"

I set down my fork on the small plate. "Well, maybe because we both work all the time, and it's impossible for us to find time to actually go out and have lunch like normal friends?" We'd wanted to try this new tea room a little north of the Cove for several months now, but it was hard to find a date when both of us were free.

Emmy nodded. "Yup, you're probably right. We need to stop doing that, the working all the time."

"I don't see that happening any time soon."

She shrugged. "I don't know. Cooper's insisting that I

need to slow down. I told him I'm not giving up the weekends at the Tide, and I don't want to stop making pies." Sighing, she snagged another piece of scone from her plate. "But I might have to compromise. The man wants more time with me, and how the hell am I supposed to argue with that?"

"You're not." I fiddled with the edge of my napkin, rolling it between two of my fingers. "You've found the one, Em. Maybe it's time to relax a little and let him take care of you."

She snorted. "I'm not sure I remember how to do that. I've been taking care of me—and then three little mini-mes—for so long, I don't think I can stop."

"Cooper loves you. Part of loving you means keeping you healthy and sane. And if that means slowing down, and letting him do for you a little . . . why not? You deserve it, my friend. All that and much more."

"Hmmm." Emmy steepled her fingers and eyed me. "Well, since turnabout is fair play, what about you? When are you going to slow down?"

"Not any time soon. Besides, I don't have anyone who cares that I work so much."

"No?" She lifted her water glass to take a sip. "That's odd. I could've sworn maybe there was something you're not telling me." She set down the glass and looked at me expectantly.

I felt the heat creep up my cheeks. "Like what?"

"Oh, that maybe there's a certain contractor—excuse me, restoration specialist—who's interested in more than just your studs?"

"My studs? Really, Em?"

She giggled. "I know, lousy metaphor. Sue me, I know nothing about construction. But stop trying to change the subject. What's going on with you and Ryland?"

I tried for an innocent expression, my eyes wide. "I don't know what you're talking about. We work together. That's it."

"Oh, really? Then want to tell me why he was sneaking up to your apartment last night in the middle of the band's first set?"

Damn. "I'm sure he wasn't sneaking up there, Emmy. Ryland had a question for me, and I answered it." That wasn't a lie. I was fairly certain he'd asked me some question at some point, even if it had had more to do with kissing and less to do with work.

"Uh huh. And was that question, 'Will you do me now, Abby?'" She snickered.

"You're so vulgar. No, in fact, it wasn't. There was no . . . doing of anyone." I folded my napkin in a small square. "Now can we change the subject? You're bringing down the tone of our sophisticated ladies lunch."

"I'm just trying to get at the truth. You might remember, my friend, that you told me how hurt you were last spring because I didn't tell you about Cooper and me. So I'm sure if you're getting down and dirty with the contractor dude, you would tell me. Right?"

I squirmed. Emmy wasn't wrong. I'd whined about her not coming clean, and now I was hedging.

"There hasn't been any down and dirty. I swear. But there may have been . . . kissing." I was sure my face was pink. "You can't tell anyone, though, Emmy. We want to keep it quiet while we're working together."

"Do you really think Jude and Logan would care about that?" She rolled her eyes and waved her hand. "Jude would be the first one to tell you to go for it."

"Still." I leaned back. "I don't know exactly what's going on between us. Maybe it's going to be nothing. So I don't want to make a big deal, okay? If it looks like we're going to elope, I promise I'll tell you first."

"You better. I have dibs on matron of honor." Emmy reached across to pat my hand. "Abby, do you like him? Ryland, I mean? *Like* him, like him?"

"Sorry, I didn't realize we were back in middle school." I gave her a little nudge with my foot under the table. "I like Ryland, yes. Satisfied?"

"Are you in love with him?"

I shook my head. "Too early, Em. We've only just acknowledged we like kissing each other. I'm not rushing into anything. I've learned my lesson there."

"I understand." She hesitated. "Abby, would you tell me what happened in Boston?"

I sagged against the chair. I'd told myself that if Emmy or Jude ever asked me point-blank, I'd tell them. Neither of them had until now.

"I made a crucial error in judgment." I chewed on the corner of my lip. "It was my first solo managing job, and I let myself get swept away by the guy who was the assistant manager at the restaurant." I closed my eyes, remembering, waiting for the pain to sweep over me again. Oddly, it didn't hurt as much as it had. "He told me he loved me. He wanted to marry me. We made plans. And then it turned out it was all lies. He only wanted me for how far I could get him in my father's company, and my father found out."

"Jesus, Ab." Emmy's forehead was furrowed, her eyes worried. "That's horrible. I'm so sorry."

"It was humiliating because I screwed up my job and lost the position. And my heart was broken, because it was with Zachary that I really opened up for the first time. I loved him, Emmy. And he didn't love me. He pretended, and when I found out it was all a joke to him—I didn't ever want to get out of bed again."

"I don't blame you." Emmy twisted her napkin in her hands. "I remember when Eddy ran off, I felt that way. I didn't love him by then, not really, but I was mortified that I'd let him put me in that position. When I found out how much Matt had been helping us all along, paying Eddy extra, I wanted to curl up and die. It felt like everyone in town knew what a loser I'd married. Everyone but me." She leaned forward. "But then I got angry. I got good and pissed. And you know what? That got me moving."

I pressed my hands to my face. "I don't think I ever got mad at Zachary. Maybe because I did love him still, and the broken heart trumped the mad. And then when I got the offer for the Hawthorne House, I just ran." I drew in a ragged breath. "It took me months before I'd even see my father again. I let him down, and I embarrassed him, too."

"Bullshit. You got taken in by a liar and a dickhead. There's no crime in trusting, Ab. And I hope you won't let this Zachary jerk keep you from giving Ryland a chance. From what I can see, he's a good guy. He gave Lacie Barnet the boot last night when she was painting herself all over him, and that gave him a gold star in my book."

"Oh, it was Lacie coming on to him? He told me about it, but I didn't know who." Lacie was very pretty, with big boobs and a smile that seemed to draw men to her. Ryland definitely got points for turning her down.

"Yup. She was pissed, too." Emmy shook her head, smiling, and then squeezed my hand again. "Thank you, Abby, for trusting me enough to tell me about Boston and Zachary. I'm sorry it happened, but on the other hand, if it hadn't, you wouldn't have ended up in the Cove, right?"

"True." I hadn't considered that. At first, the Cove had just been a place to hide and heal. Eventually, it had become home, but I'd never thought about the fact that if it weren't for Zachary, I might still have been in Boston, or managing some other cookie-cutter Donavan hotel somewhere else in the world. Maybe I owed him a debt of gratitude after all.

The waiter appeared with our check, which we'd agreed to split. I slid my credit card from its spot in my wallet and tucked it into the pocket on the folder.

"How did you find this job, anyway?" Emmy dug into her purse, looking for her card. "I don't remember Jude and Logan advertising for the position at the Hawthorne House."

"You know, I'm not really sure. It was weird. I just got an email from Logan one day, telling me about the job and asking if I might be interested. I didn't have any other options, so I said yes, fast. I'm so glad I did."

"Me, too. Still, I wonder how he got your name." Emmy found her credit card and slapped it on the folder next to mine. "God, I need to clean out this purse. So do you think your dad told Logan about you?"

I frowned. "No. My father was insisting I needed to go back to Philadelphia and work under him for another year or two. And that was the last thing I wanted to do." I paused. "I have a complicated relationship with my parents. My parents split up when I was thirteen. My sister was six. She went with my mom, and I chose to stay with my father, because I thought he needed me. I was mad at my mom for breaking up what I thought was a perfect family. Turned out she was just trying to save herself from a man who was bent on self-destruction."

"Oh, honey. I'm sorry."

I had never told anyone about my family or about my parents' divorce, but now, having pulled the cork, it all came spilling out. "I found out a few years later that my dad was a serial cheater. He never could manage that whole being faithful thing. And he's an alcoholic." I swallowed hard. "I had to fly up there a few months ago because his current wife left him, and he was making a mess of his life. Again."

Emmy sat still for a moment, studying me. "What about your mother? Are you close to her?"

"Not as much as I'd like. I spent some holidays with her growing up, but after she got married again, it was hard."

"You didn't like her new husband?"

I laughed, a brief, mirthless sound. "Actually, the opposite. Geoffrey is wonderful. He adores my mother, he treats my sister Jess like his own and he's always been great to me. But it felt like I was betraying my father whenever I enjoyed time with my mother and Geoffrey. So I wasn't always the nicest person when I was around them growing up."

"Abby." Emmy held my hand. "You can't blame yourself for acting like a child when you were one. I'm sure your mother understood."

"She was always very patient. And now we have a civil relationship. We talk on the phone once or twice a month, and I try to see them at least once a year. I think she'd like more, but I haven't been able to manage it. Maybe someday."

The waiter reappeared to run our cards and returned with the receipts. I bit my lip as I signed the paper, as the sense that I'd shared too much broke over me. I didn't talk about private family matters. I'd never told any of my friends growing up about my parents' divorce; most of them didn't know I had a sister. And now Emmy would pity me, and I couldn't stand that.

We walked out toward her car in silence. She'd driven us to the tearoom, but now I was regretting not bringing my own car as Emmy navigated us onto the road that led back to Crystal Cove. I needed a minute to recover, to get back to feeling like I had some modicum of control.

"Abby, I know you're an intensely private person. I am, too. I think that's why we hit it off so well when we met. It's important for me to take care of myself and never admit I need help. Drives Cooper crazy, and I never got it. But I think I do now." We stopped at a red light, and she turned toward me. "The fact that you told me about your family makes me feel like you trust me. It makes me feel like we really are friends, and the next time I'm at the end of my rope and need someone, I'll feel safe calling you. Because you trusted me, I can trust you. So thank you for opening that door in our friendship."

I let out the breath I'd been holding. "Really? You're not sitting there feeling sorry for me, thinking how pathetic I am, even though I make a big deal of being in control?"

Emmy snorted. "No, I'm thinking how brave you are, and how hard it must be for you to open up and trust someone, and how honored I am that you let me in."

Relief and gratitude filled me. "Thank you, Emmy. I'm glad you're my friend. I'm even a little grateful to Zachary for breaking my heart and ruining my career so that I ended up here with you."

"That's what we call growth. But don't give the jerk too much credit. Hey, do you mind if we stop at Cooper's real fast? I've had this piece of driftwood from Jude in the back of my car for almost a week. I keep forgetting to drop it off to him, and he keeps forgetting to get it out of my trunk. We're going to go right past his workshop."

"Sure, no problem. What's he doing with it?"

Emmy grinned. "He's making a table for Jude to give to Logan for their anniversary. Can you believe it's three years already?"

"That's crazy. Seems like just yesterday I got here and met the two of them. They weren't together yet. Do you remember the party where they told all of us that they were seeing each other?"

"Like it was yesterday. And their wedding?"

"So beautiful. We both cried." I nudged Emmy. "So am I going to be crying at another wedding any time soon?"

"Ha! Not unless it's yours, baby girl." Emmy hooked a left turn into the gravel lot between Cooper's house and the oversized garage that served as his workshop. "Come in with me and say hello."

She didn't need to ask me twice. I loved Coop's work-shop; it smelled of sawdust and stain and old wood, and it was filled with beautiful pieces in various states of comple-tion. The place was a little piece of nirvana for me.

Emmy pushed open the door, and I followed her inside. We always entered cautiously, so as not to startle Cooper in case he was using a saw or some other sharp tool that could maim him. But there was no whine of the jigsaw today; in-stead I could hear men's voices. And I recognized one of them.

"Hey, beautiful." Cooper broke away from the conver-sation and reached for Emmy. He pulled her tight, kissing her in a way that made me feel a little like a voyeur. "Thanks for bringing this by." He slung his arm around her shoulder and drew her forward, smiling at me as he did. "Hi, Abby. Good to see you. Em, you know Ryland. This is Lincoln Turner."

"Yeah, I know. We met last night at the Tide. Hey, Ry-land." Emmy shot a quick glance at me.

"Emmy, Abby." Ryland was leaning against the tool bench, his long legs stretched out in front of him. He met my eyes, and a shot of pure heat hit me, stealing my breath. It felt like an electric current was running between us, and it was with tremendous effort that I tore my gaze away.

"Hello, Mr. Kent." I reverted to my old standby. "And Mr. Turner, how nice to meet you at last. I've heard wonder-ful things about your work." I leaned forward and offered my hand to the other man. He wasn't quite as tall as Ry-land, and he was definitely older. Something in his grey eyes spoke of a weary pain. I wondered what it was.

"You must be Ms. Donavan." I didn't miss the glance Linc slid toward Ryland. "You're as lovely as I've heard. And congratulations on the Riverside. It's a beautiful place, and I'm sure it's going to thrive under you."

"That's the plan." I let myself look at Ryland again, just for a minute. God, he was handsome. I remembered the way his lips had felt against mine last night, his hands pressing my back so that I'd felt the unmistakable evidence of his arousal. I forced my attention back to his friend. "So you're estimating we can open in six to eight weeks?"

"Yeah, that's what I think." Linc frowned. "Where did you hear that?"

Crap. Ryland had mentioned the timeline last night while he was at my apartment. I opened my mouth to come up with some sort of explanation when Emmy came to my rescue.

"Ryland told me last night at the Tide, and Abby and I talked about it today. You don't know the Cove yet, but word travels fast."

I smiled at her in gratitude and in awe. She hadn't lied, but she'd covered my ass and Ryland's. Emmy Carter was one smart chick.

"Well, I better go pick up the kids at my parents' house. Mom keeps complaining she never sees them anymore, now that Cooper's in the picture, but I don't want to overtax her, either." Emmy kissed Cooper's cheek and sketched a wave to the other men. "Boys, try to behave yourselves. No cutting off any important body parts. Abby, you ready?"

"Um, yes." I jerked my attention away from Ryland.

"See you tomorrow, Mr. Kent. Mr. Turner."

"Yup." Linc gave me a brief nod, and Ryland mumbled something I couldn't decipher.

We were halfway across the parking lot when I heard my name. "Abby! Hold up a minute."

Ryland was jogging after us. Emmy grinned at me and kept walking. "I'll just be in the car. Take your time."

I turned and waited for him, my arms crossed over my chest. "What can I do for you, Mr. Kent?"

One side of his mouth turned up. "I love it when you call me that."

I chewed the inside of my bottom lip to keep from smiling back at him. "Did you need something?"

"Yeah. Yeah, I did. I do." Ryland hauled me against his hard body, tipping my chin up until my lips were just below his. "God, I wanted to do this as soon as I saw you in there." He slanted his open mouth over mine, kissing me with more urgency and aggression than he had the night before. I wriggled against him, my heart pounding as I tried to get even closer. My breasts were crushed against his chest, and the muscles there teased my nipples erect through the silk of my blouse and my bra.

"Ryland." I tore my mouth away. "Anyone could walk by. And Linc's right inside."

"I know." He ran his hands down my back and gripped my ass. "Right now I don't give a damn."

"Right now. But later you will." I let my head fall against his shoulder. "Did you come out just for this?"

"If I had, it'd be worth it. But actually, I came out here to ask you to dinner."

I drew back so that I could look up into his eyes. "Dinner?"

"Yeah, it's the meal at the end of day. Are you familiar with it?"

"Yes, smarty pants. I know what you mean. But why? And when?"

He eased away from me but kept his hands at my hips. "Why, because I want to take you on a date. A real date, where I pick you up, and we eat together, and then I walk you to your door and kiss you good-night." He bent his head down to whisper in my ear. "I might even try to cop a feel. Just a warning."

"What happened to laying low and not telling anyone about us until the hotel's done?"

Ryland shook his head. "I'm taking you to a restaurant out of the Cove. But that's mostly because I want you to be able to relax and not worry about running into people you know. I want you to be Abby, not Ms. Donavan."

"Hmm. Okay." I tilted my head. "So when?"

"Friday. I'll pick you up at six-thirty."

Friday seemed like a very long time away. "All right. Do you have other hot dates lined up for the rest of the week?"

He laughed. "Yeah, and they're all with Linc. We have to finalize the plans for the detail work and take care of some paperwork for the company. He'll be sick of me by Friday night. And I thought it'd be good for you to be out of your apartment on one of the loud nights."

"It's sweet of you to remember that. I'll be looking forward to it."

Ryland chuckled and kissed the tip of my nose. "That's

my Ms. Donavan right there."

I frowned. "What do you mean?"

"Most girls would say something like, 'Awesome, I'll be ready.' Sometimes you talk like you just stepped out of a PBS special."

"I'm . . . sorry?"

"Don't be. I think it's hot." He glanced over his shoulder. "I better get back inside. We're going over the fixtures for all the cabinetry."

"Okay. I'm sure I'll see you at the hotel tomorrow."

"I'll be in the stables tomorrow. Oh, excuse me." He winked. "I mean, the spa. We're finishing the dry-walling."

"I'll be sure to stop by." As I turned back toward the car, Ryland called me once more.

"Abby, by the way, I told Cooper to cancel the shutters for the dining room. You're right. I overstepped."

Part of me wanted to run and hug him, but instead I drew myself up and inclined my head. "Thank you, Mr. Kent. I appreciate you seeing things my way."

Ryland grinned. "Oooh, baby. Don't tease me like that." He blew me a kiss and opened the door to the workshop.

I made my way back to the car and climbed into the passenger seat. "Oh, Emmy. I think I'm in trouble."

chapter nine

Ryland

FOR A SOLID WEEK, I had the worst case of blue balls I'd ever known.

It started on Monday morning. I'd come onto the job site early in the hope that Abby would come by, too. I wasn't disappointed. I'd just started taping the dry wall when I heard the familiar sound of her heels clicking toward me.

"Good morning, Mr. Kent." Her voice was the same, distant and formal. But the whole effect was destroyed by the smile that quirked up one side of her mouth. And when I got a look at her, I nearly swallowed my tongue. She was wearing one of her flirty little skirts, pairing it with cotton tank that hugged her tits. It was topped with a sweater, but that didn't hide the swell of cleavage.

"Donavan, you look so fucking hot this morning." I spoke deliberately, just to see the flush of pink steal over her cheeks. Sure enough, there it was.

"Thank you for the compliment. I think." She glanced around the large space that would eventually be the quiet room for the Riverside Spa. "Where is everyone?"

"Detail crew starts in the main building this morning, and Linc's overseeing that. The local guys are working in here, but they won't begin for another twenty minutes or so." I brushed dust off my shirt and reached to snag Abby's hand. "That means we're alone." Drawing her closer, I slid my fingers under her sweater, just grazing the undersides of her boobs as I kissed her lips.

Fifteen minutes later, the first workmen arrived on the site, passing a slightly-disheveled and flustered boss lady. They may also have wondered why I couldn't stand up for the next ten minutes.

That was how the week went: stolen kisses whenever we were alone, a little more groping each time we were together, all interspersed with our regular meetings, during which we both pretended that nothing had changed between us. But each time Abby called me 'Mr. Kent', I wanted to throw her down on the floor and kiss her senseless.

By the time we got to Friday, I couldn't wait to get Abby alone, and not just because I wanted to touch her. I realized I wanted to talk to her about more than just the hotel. I wanted to find out more about her, tell her about me. I wanted to hear her laugh, and I wanted to see her blush.

I left the hotel a little late when I was held up by the electrician. Once we were finished, I had just enough time to grab a shower and get dressed. Linc caught me as I was buttoning my shirt.

"Well, aren't you fancy tonight? What's the rush, Casanova?"

I had decided that I wasn't going to lie to Lincoln about my relationship with Abby. He wouldn't like it, probably, but we'd always been honest with each other. On the other hand, I didn't have to blab it all out at once if he didn't actually ask.

"Going out." I tucked my shirt into the waistband of my pants.

"I didn't figure you'd dressed up to spend a quiet night at home with me. Where're you heading? Not the Tide, huh?"

"No."

"So you're taking our lady boss out of town to wine and dine her?"

"Yeah, I—wait, what? How did you know?" I gaped at Lincoln. Here I'd been sneaking around all week, thinking I was being stealthy, and he'd figured it out?

He laughed. "Ry, buddy, I wasn't born yesterday. You think I missed the sparks between the two of you last weekend at Cooper's workshop? Or how you sprinted out after her when she left? Or the lipstick on your neck every day after you leave the outbuildings and come into the main hotel?" He shook his head. "I'm not stupid or blind, dude."

I fastened the cuffs on my shirt. "Are you pissed at me?"

"Ryland, I'm not your father or your boss. I'm not even your partner. I can tell you I think it's a bad idea to get involved with the client, but I can't fire you. I can't ground you. You gotta do what you think is right." He paused. "And she's pretty cool. I have to admit it. She's tough, yeah, but she knows what she's doing, and she's fair."

"So I have your blessing?"

Linc smirked. "I thought we just established you don't need my blessing. But if you want it, then sure." He hesitated, as though he wanted to say more. "Just be careful, okay, man? The lady boss isn't one of your typical girls. She's all about long term and forevers, if you haven't noticed. Don't mess with her if you're just looking for a quickie, okay?"

"I'm way ahead of you, Linc. I know Abby isn't an easy lay. And I don't want that with her." I rubbed my jaw. "I don't know about forever. We haven't known each other very long. But she's the first woman I've ever met where I can see the possibility of . . . longer. Does that make sense?"

"Yup. And I'm happy for you, Ry." He glanced at the clock. "Now you better haul ass or you're going to be late to pick her up and she'll freeze you with her ice stare."

But there wasn't any ice in sight when I climbed the steps to Abby's apartment again. The dinner crowd was still there in force at the Tide, and I waved to Emmy as I walked through the dining room. I didn't miss the arch smile on her face, but I chose to ignore it.

I didn't have to beat on the door tonight. I knocked lightly, and the door swung open. And for the space of several minutes, I forgot to breathe.

She was wearing a dress in a shade of green that exactly matched her eyes. The material clung to her breasts below the rounded neckline before falling into a skirt that ended several inches above her knees. Of course she was wearing heels. I had a sudden image of Abby on her back, legs wrapped around my waist as her high heel shoes dug into my skin. I hoped the swell between my legs didn't show.

She'd left her hair down, and it shimmered around her shoulders, the ends teasing her pale skin left bare by the straps of her dress.

"My God, Abby." I reached one finger to touch her cheek, as though I were afraid she might break. "You're gorgeous. I've never seen a more beautiful woman in my life."

She blushed, and suddenly she was even more breathtaking. "Thank you. You look very handsome, too. Just let me grab my sweater, and I'll be right with you."

I stood on the landing as she locked the door to her apartment and then hesitated. "Do you want me to go down first, and then you come in a little bit? So people don't see us together?"

I swallowed a laugh. "Abby, darlin', there's just your apartment up here. If people see us come down together or separately, they're going to figure out we were both in here. I say let's throw caution to the wind and walk down together."

She smiled, drew in a deep breath, and offered me her hand. I clasped it firmly in mine and led her down the steps.

I helped her into my truck—having to give her a boost while holding her hips was definitely not a hardship—and then jogged around to my own seat. We headed out of the Cove and into the fading light of dusk.

"Lincoln knows about us." I hadn't meant to blurt out the words, but I wanted Abby to be aware of it. "He figured it out this week."

"Was he mad?" She crossed her legs and the skirt of her dress fluttered, riding up and showing me her inner thigh.

Damn.

"No. He just told me to be careful. He likes you."

"Does he? I'm glad. I like him, too." She brushed the hair off her shoulders, and the movement sent an intoxicating scent drifting my way. "How long have you known Linc?"

I smiled. "For ten years. I met him on my very first job, just out of vocational school. I was this cocky kid, and Linc knew what he was doing. I was smart enough to stick by him and watch. He took me under his wing, and brought me home to introduce me to his wife. Once that happened, they started to feed me. A few jobs, I actually lived with them."

"Linc's married?"

I sighed. "Widowed. Four years now."

"Oh, my God, I'm sorry. She must have been very young."

I navigated the entrance to the highway. "She was. And very cool. Funny, smart, and kind." I glanced at Abby. "You remind me of Sylvia a little. Though you're a little more . . . contained than she was."

"Contained? Is that another way of saying I'm cold?" She was teasing me, I could tell, so I played along.

"Nope. Just that you keep all that heat shut up until you're ready to unleash it."

She smiled. "I've never been accused of running hot. So Linc's been alone since his wife died?"

"Sort of." I glanced at Abby. "He kind of went off the rails after her accident."

"She was killed in a car accident?"

"Yeah. They think she fell asleep at the wheel. Her car went over a bridge." I swallowed over the lump that always rose in my throat when I remembered those bleak days. "It was horrible. Thank God the kids were home with her parents."

"Oh, they had children?" The dismay in Abby's voice was real.

"Becca and Oliver. They're the greatest kids." I paused, checking to see how close we were to the exit I needed to take. "Linc had just gotten a job close to home, something that would keep him in one place. No more travel. I gave him a hard time about it, but I knew it was what he needed to do for his family. I didn't have that, so traveling was never a big deal. He was on the last project we were doing together, and Sylvia had gone to see her parents. She left the kids with them and ran out to pick up dinner, and I guess she was so tired from the drive in . . . Linc blamed himself."

Abby's eyebrows drew together. "Why? It wasn't his fault."

"No, it wasn't, but he felt like if he'd been home by then, she wouldn't have been driving." I eased over one lane, checking the mirrors. Talking about Sylvia's accident made me hyper-aware of my own driving safety. "Linc couldn't handle everything once she was gone. He started drinking, and everything went downhill from there."

"That's terrible." There wasn't judgment in Abby's voice, just sadness. "But things are better now?"

"Yeees." In many ways, Linc had recovered. But I knew part of him never would. Part of his heart had died that day with Sylvia. "I mean, he doesn't drink anymore. He's in a twelve-step program, and he's been sober for almost three years. But Sylvia's parents took custody of the kids when he was drinking, and they still have them. Linc hasn't fought to change that. I think part of him feels like he failed them, and he doesn't deserve to have them back."

"Would he have to go to court?"

"No, nothing was ever done formally or legally. Linc goes to see the kids as often as he can, between jobs, and technically, he could take them any time. But his in-laws have convinced him that moving Becca and Oliver would hurt them at this point. So he's just miserable all the time." I took the next exit. "We're almost there. Are you hungry?"

"Starving." Abby grinned. "I was too nervous to eat lunch today."

I loved that she was comfortable enough with me to admit that. "Why were you nervous? We've kind of done things backwards. You don't have to worry about our first kiss or that we won't have anything to talk about."

"Still." She flipped her hands over on her lap. "I tend to clam up in new situations. And dating . . ." She looked out the side window. "I haven't done much of it. I had one semi-serious boyfriend in high school, and a few first dates here and there. And then Zachary. So I always worry I'm lacking some basic ability to handle this kind of situation."

"Hey." I captured her hand and squeezed it. "Don't think about tonight that way. It's just you, Abby, and me, Ryland, eating dinner together. Nothing scary. Just the two of us and some amazing Asian food."

"Asian?" Her voice rose in what I hoped was anticipation.

"Yeah. I might've done a little recon. And Emmy might've told me that you believe the one thing the Cove's missing is a really good Asian restaurant." I slowed the truck and turned down a tree-lined road. "Cooper told me this place is a hidden gem. I hope he's right."

The trees gave way to a more open, busier street, and when we came to a small strip-mall, I pulled into the parking lot. Just as Coop had warned me, from the outside, the place didn't look like much. I stole a quick glance at Abby to see if she was having second thoughts. But no, she wore a huge smile.

"This is perfect." She gathered her handbag and opened the truck door. "All the best Asian food comes from little places like this. When I lived in the Bay Area, I used to go to a restaurant in Oakland that looked like this. I'd order a few dishes, take home the leftovers and eat well for a week."

I met her on the passenger side of the truck and caught both her hands in mine. "You're pretty damn amazing, you know that, Abby Donavan?"

She looked up at me, eyes glowing and lips curved. "Is that a good thing?"

"It's a wonderful thing." I pulled her closer, moving her hands around my body to meet behind my back, forcing her flush against me. When I bent my head to capture her lips, she made a small noise at the back of her throat that made me want to turn around and push her up on the side of my truck. Instead, I opened my mouth and coaxed her tongue between my lips, not touching her anywhere else as I held her hands captive in mine.

"What was this for?" She murmured the words against my lips. "I thought the kiss came after we ate, when you took me home."

"I couldn't wait." The confession was spontaneous. "So now the pressure's off. We can relax and enjoy dinner, knowing that the kiss is out of the way."

Abby thrust out her lower lip in a pretend pout. "So that's the only kiss I'm getting tonight?"

I laughed, released her hands and gave her a gentle shove toward the door of the restaurant. "Not if you play your cards right."

The inside of the Mandarin Court wasn't anything special. The man who showed us to our table smiled widely as he handed us laminated menus and filled our water glasses; I noticed that just about every table was occupied, which was probably a good sign. Abby appeared to be completely at ease, flipping through the pages and muttering as her finger tapped on one picture and then another.

"What looks good?" I glanced down the list of dinner specials. "I'm a boring Chinese food customer. I usually just order beef and broccoli."

Abby's eyes widened, and she shook her head. "Don't tell me such things. All of the wonderful choices, and you always get the same thing. What a waste!" She cocked her head, considering me. "Do you trust me, Ryland?"

Every time she said my name, a jolt of desire shot straight to my cock. "Uh, yeah. I do."

"All right. Let me order for us then. I promise, you won't be sorry."

When the waiter appeared, Abby closed her menu and began firing off requests with rapid-fire precision, using her hands as she asked questions and smiling when he nodded enthusiastically. I wasn't sure I understood most of their exchange, but I could tell we weren't going to be getting Special Meal Number Two.

"Were you speaking Chinese there?" I sipped my water, raising one eyebrow.

Abby shrugged. "A little bit of Mandarin, and little Yue."

"Yue? Never heard of it."

"You'd call it Cantonese."

"Oh, really?" I reached across the table and threaded my fingers into Abby's. "And how did you pick up that ability?"

"I told you we lived in the Bay Area for a while. The manager of the Donavan San Francisco was a Chinese man with a huge family. After my mom . . . left, he and his wife Corrine sort of adopted me into their life. They were my auntie and uncle." She spoke with the kind of affection I didn't hear often in her voice.

"Do you see them very much these days?"

Abby nodded. "Whenever I can. I always stop and spend a few days with them when I visit my mom in Napa. Uncle Edwin is the one who taught me how to order in Mandarin. They'd take me to Dim Sum, and Auntie Corrine would order so fast, I couldn't keep up, but he made sure I learned the words. And then I knew a girl in college who spoke Yue, and so I picked that dialect up from her." She shook her head a little. "I can't really speak it, but I know how to order food."

"And that's a valuable skill to have." I paused a minute, trying to think of the best way to frame my next question. "You said your mom left, and I realized I've never heard you really talk about her much, only your father. Are you close to her?"

152

Something flickered in Abby's eyes. "We have a decent relationship, but no, we're not close. When she left my dad, she took my younger sister Jessica with her, and I elected to stay with my father. I think I hurt her, and it's taken years to get over that." She hesitated and ran the tip of her tongue over her bottom lip. "When I found out that my dad had been cheating on her and drinking all the time, I wanted to leave. To go apologize to my mother and beg her to forgive me for not understanding before. But by then I was sixteen, and she'd just remarried. I was too stubborn to admit I'd been wrong about my father, so instead I stayed with him, covered for him . . . and was miserable."

I flipped my hand so that hers lay within mine, moving my fingers to caress her palm. "That sucks. And you've never talked with her about it?"

She shook her head. "No, we're not that kind of family. We smile, and we pretend everything's fine." She glanced up at me, her eyes troubled. "You think I'm closed off—well, you called it 'contained'. But that's the only way I've known how to be. It's only been in the last few years, working in the Cove and getting to be friends with Jude and Emmy, that I've realized there's another way."

I chuckled. "You'll have to come meet my family someday, Abby. No one pretends, and nothing is contained. Ever. Sometimes I used to wish it would be." I remembered some embarrassing discussions around the dinner table, growing up. "You'll appreciate your parents after that."

"I doubt it." She moved her fingers around my wrist, her nails scraping just enough to be slightly erotic. "Are your parents still married?"

"Oh, yeah, thirty years and counting. My sisters and I pretend it's not big deal, but it's nice to know our folks are still in love. My dad can't stand it when Mom goes away without him, and my mother gets up every morning to make Dad breakfast before work."

"Do your sisters still live in New Jersey?"

I nodded. "Yup, they all live within about fifteen minutes of each other. I have three nieces and two nephews, and my mom's always pestering me to settle down and give her more grandchildren. It's so stereotypical, it's disgusting."

"It sounds wonderful." I couldn't miss the wistful note in Abby's voice. "Why did you leave?"

I blew out a breath. "I felt like I was smothering there. I knew I didn't want to go to a four-year college, but I didn't want a dead-end contractor job, either. My grandfather was a restoration hobbyist—you know, someone who just does a little work on the side, not as a main job. He taught me some, and he introduced me to a guy who ran a company out of Kansas City. I went to vocational school for a few years, and then I started at the bottom of Leo's business. That's where I met Linc."

"And eventually you started your own company?"

"Yeah. It was already in the works when Sylvia died. I'd wanted Linc to come on as my partner, but he turned me down so he could stay home with his family. And then . . . after, I offered him partnership again, but he'd just stopped drinking, and he didn't want the pressure. So for now, at least, we're keeping things as they are."

A rattle of glass across the room caught my attention, and my mouth dropped open as three waiters marched toward our table, each carrying a tray. A fourth one hurried to open stands, beaming at us as they all began to deposit food in front of us.

"Good God, woman!" I looked at Abby in alarm. "How are we going to eat all this?"

She laughed, clapping her hands in delight, and for a moment, she looked so young and carefree that I wanted to freeze time.

"We won't! But just think of the fun we'll have enjoying the leftovers." She snatched up a pair of chopsticks, her eyes sparkling at me. "Did I mention I always eat my take-home Chinese food in bed?"

I had a sudden and vivid image of Abby, surrounded by white containers, wearing nothing but a sultry smile as she ate lo mein with chop sticks.

"Oh, baby." I groaned the words, making her laugh even harder. "I think I just found a whole new appreciation for leftovers."

"I swear to God, Abby, I can't eat another bite." I leaned back in the booth. "You've won. You out-ate me. Just roll me out and let me die."

"Ryland." Abby shook her head. "You disappoint me. Come on, you have to at least have one fortune cookie." She cracked one open and squinted at the miniscule type on the slip of paper. "'You will find much happiness and satisfaction with someone most unexpected . . . in bed.'" She glanced up at me, speculation in her eyes. "Hmmmm."

"It does not say that. Let me see." I held out my hand, but Abby kept it out of reach, giggling.

"It does say that. Well, sort of. It's a game we always played in college. You add the words 'in bed' to your fortune." She winked at me. "Makes them more fun."

I rolled my eyes. "What is it with you and Chinese food and bed? I'm starting to think . . ." I broke off when her face went bright red. "Oh, that's it, isn't it?" I lowered my voice. "Did you have a fling that had something to do with Chinese food? Like, lots of food?"

Abby covered her face. "Oh, God. This is embarrassing." She peeked at me through her fingers. "Okay, yes. My first time to . . . well, my first time was with a guy I met through my auntie's son. His family owned a restaurant in Chinatown, and I was always getting food delivered. Mostly because I loved what they made, but also because I had a huge crush on Tyler."

I sat back, smirking. "Uh huh. So you and Tyler did the nasty while you were having your leftovers in bed?"

"Nooooo." She shook her head. "It wasn't exactly like that. I took him to my prom in senior year, and afterwards we stopped at his parents' restaurant and took food back to my suite at the hotel, and well . . . one thing led to another."

"You slut, you." I teased her, just to see if I could get her to blush again.

"Hardly." Abby crumpled the clear cellophane from the cookie in her fist. "After Tyler, there was one guy in my senior year of college, and then no one else until Zachary. I'm no expert, but I think three lovers does not a slut make."

"You haven't been with a man since Zachary? Wasn't that, like, three years ago?" I couldn't imagine. A woman like Abby? Why hadn't some other guy snatched her up?

"No. I don't exactly troll bars for men to pick up, and my work hasn't lent itself to meeting many single straight men." She caught the corner of her lip between her teeth. "And I wasn't looking. I've been healing, I guess."

"Until a certain irresistible, drop-dead handsome, smart and sexy restoration specialist swept into your life and made you realize how much you'd been missing." I gave her a mock leer. "You lucky girl."

A lazy smile spread over her full lips. "Take this lucky girl home before she falls into a food coma, please."

We rode home in companionable silence, talking more about our mutual friends than ourselves. Abby made me laugh as she described the night last spring when Jude and Logan had pretended to try to fix her up with Cooper.

"It was hysterical and awful at the same time." She leaned back in the passenger seat, curling up her knees and stretching the skirt of her dress over her legs. "Cooper walked in, saw me, and immediately smelled a set up. I knew the score, of course—Jude wanted to make Cooper and Emmy admit they were seeing each other. But I had to pretend to be interested in Cooper." She giggled. "Don't get me wrong, Cooper's a wonderful man, but I knew he only had eyes for Em."

"Why didn't they want to tell anyone?" I knew Cooper and Emmy hadn't been living together very long, but I hadn't realized how new their relationship was.

"They wouldn't admit it to each other. Coop had a few

bad marriages and thought he was doomed to failure when it came to relationships. Emmy was still leery after her husband left her. They kept pretending they were just hooking up." Abby sighed. "I wanted to knock their heads together and made them see the truth, but Jude said that would be counter-productive."

"I'd think so." I turned onto the main street of Crystal Cove. It was quiet for a Friday night; most of the locals were already in for the evening, and there was a lull in tourist traffic. "Cooper and Emmy were gun-shy, huh?"

"Yes, I guess so."

I pulled into the jammed parking lot outside the Riptide and maneuvered the truck into the yellow no parking zone near the building. One of the perks of working for the owners was the fact that I didn't have to worry about getting towed.

Shifting the truck into neutral, I turned in my seat to face Abby. I'd noticed that the closer we'd gotten to her apartment, the more withdrawn she'd become. Now she sat still, staring through the windshield. I ventured one finger to trace the line of her cheek.

"Abby?" My voice was low, intimate. I saw the movement of her throat as she swallowed. "Are you still scared?"

She flashed a glance in my direction. "Yes." The word came out on a rush of breath before her chest lifted as she spoke again. "But I'm not terrified anymore."

I smiled, her honesty as always disarming me. "Well, that's something."

One corner of her lips turned up just a little. "I'm not afraid of you, Ryland. But I'm still scared of what could happen between us, and how it could affect me."

I nodded. "I won't push you, Abby. We move at your speed. And I promise I'll always tell you the truth. I'm not looking for anything from you. I don't want a job or your money or even just your cooperation on the hotel job." I let my fingers stroke down the side of her neck. "I only want you."

She leaned into my hand, her eyes drifting shut. "Do you want to come upstairs?"

God, did I want to. Each time I'd held her this week, kissing her senseless in the shadowed corners of our job site, I'd wanted more. My dreams at night were becoming more excruciatingly detailed as my mind supplied the sound of her soft moans and the feel of her skin under my fingers. I hadn't been this turned on without doing something about it since high school.

"There's nothing I want more." I slipped my hand under the weight of her hair, rubbing the back of her neck. "But if I go up with you now, I won't want to leave. And I think we're not ready for that yet."

I felt the sag of her muscles as she relaxed a little. "I want to argue with you and say I am. But I'm not sure."

"We're running this train on your schedule, Donavan. It's all you. You'll tell me when you want me to come upstairs with you." I trailed my fingers down her bare arm, smiling at her shiver, and then lifted her hand to my mouth. I kissed her knuckles before I turned it over and pressed my lips to her warm palm. "But I'm going to warn you: when you do tell me you're ready, know that you're not getting rid of me any time soon."

"I'll count on that." She unfastened her seat belt. "Thank

you for a wonderful date and a delicious dinner."

She bent over to retrieve the paper bags of food at her feet, not realizing that she was giving me a tantalizing glimpse of her boobs as she did. *Oh, shit.* I started to wonder if I could backtrack on all my honorable-gentleman crap and get her to take me upstairs after all.

"I'll take these up with me, but maybe later this week, you could come over and share the leftovers with me."

"I'll count on that." I moved over toward the center of the seat. "I know I gave you a good-night kiss before dinner, but I'm thinking I should get another one now."

Abby laughed. "Oh, really? And just what makes you think you deserve a second one, Mr. Kent?"

I growled and tugged her against me, leveraging my body to loom over hers. "Baby, you know what it does to me when you call me that? Makes me want to take that second kiss, and maybe even a third and fourth."

She stilled under me. "No one has ever called me baby."

I nuzzled her throat, nipping up to just beneath her ear. "Do you find it offensive?"

The thrumming pulse beneath my lips jumped a little. "I probably should, but no. Not a bit."

"Good." I sucked lightly on the same pulse. "Because when I do get you into bed, and I'm making you come, I can't be held responsible for what I call you."

She sighed, her arms going lax around my neck. "When you say things like that, I'm not sure whether I should run away or drag you upstairs after all."

"I can tell you what my vote would be." I worked my way to her lips. "But for now, I'll settle for my second good-night kiss." I pressed my mouth to Abby's, then broke away. "And my third." This time I nudged her lips open, tracing them with the tip of my tongue. "And my fourth." Into her open mouth, I thrust my tongue, giving her a foretaste of what I was really dying to do.

When I knew I had to stop or risk never being able to, I released her, sitting up and moving back behind the wheel. "You'd better go in, Abby. It's getting late."

"Yes." She was breathless, and I knew I'd made her that way. "I can slip in before anyone notices me."

"No way you wouldn't be noticed. You're beautiful." I brushed the hair away from her eyes. "Make sure you go right upstairs, okay? I don't want to have to fight off any other guys."

"I'm not interested in any other guys." She stated it simply, matter-of-factly, but the words went straight to my heart. Without waiting for me to answer, she opened the truck door and slid to the ground, taking the leftovers with her. "Good night, Ryland. Sleep well."

I watched her climb the steps to the door of the Tide and disappear within. With a groan of frustration, I dropped my head against the headrest and closed my eyes, trying to ignore the throbbing between my legs.

I had a funny feeling sleep wasn't going to come easy tonight.

chapter ten

Abby

"**W**ELL, IF IT ISN'T MY favorite tenant slash innkeeper. I haven't seen you in a while, Abby."

I climbed onto a bar stool and gratefully accepted the mug of coffee Jude slid my way. "I know. You've been busy, and so have I been."

Jude laughed. "That sounds like an evasion if I've ever heard one."

"Not at all. All my busy is with your work, getting the hotel ready. And you were away again. I haven't left town."

"True. I ran up to see Meghan and Sam for a few days. She insisted I had to visit in the fall, when Burton does its Harvest Fest."

"Ah, and was it everything she promised?"

"It was. Logan and I had a blast. And I got to have lunch with Alex's mom, too. Oh, and I saw Rilla and Mason's baby boy. He's adorable."

I remembered Meghan's friend and bridesmaid, whom I'd met briefly at Meghan and Sam's wedding this past May. "That's wonderful."

"And apparently babies are going around. Sam's sister is pregnant, due in April."

I raised one eyebrow. "Oh, really? Anyone else have big news to share?"

Jude shook her head. "No, not Meghan. She claims she and Sam want to wait a few years. She loves her job, and I think they're enjoying the relative freedom. The farm's doing better every season. They have plenty of time." She rested her elbows on the bar. "And how are things coming at the Riverside?"

I smiled almost involuntarily. "Everything's moving on schedule. The weather's been so nice this fall, we haven't run into any issues there. Ryland and Linc think we can start planning the launch."

She quirked an eyebrow at me. "Ah. So he's Ryland now, is he?"

I glanced away. "Sorry. I didn't mean to be unprofessional."

"Abby. Really." The note of reproach in Jude's voice had me looking up in alarm. "I hope you know me better than that by now. I don't care if you call him by his first name. You might remember, I was the one who suggested the two of you would make a good couple."

When I didn't answer—like Ryland with Linc, I wasn't going to lie to Jude—she drew herself up slowly, a wide smile blossoming on her face. "Abby. You hooked up with Ryland Kent, didn't you? Good for you, girlfriend!"

I wanted to disappear into the ground. "We didn't hook up. We're just—we're seeing each other."

"Is it serious?"

I hesitated. "I think it could be. But it's still new. We're not . . . we haven't made anything official."

Jude leaned over the bar and wrapped her arms around my shoulders. "I understand. But still, that's terrific, Abby. I'm so happy for you."

"Let's not make too big a deal of this, okay? We're taking it slow. And we don't want anything between us to get in the way of the work we're doing at the hotel."

"I wouldn't expect anything less." She patted my arm. "I think I might swing by the Riverside today, if you think that's okay. I'm just dying to see how it's—oh, good morning. Can I help you?"

The bell over the door of the bar had chimed, and Jude smiled in welcome to whoever had just stepped in. But when I heard the answering voice, I nearly fell off my bar stool in shock.

"Good morning. I'm looking for Abigail Donavan. I understand she lives here. She's my daughter."

I turned in my seat, my feet tangling on the rung. "Mom? What are you doing here?"

As always, she was beautiful. Her hair was still blonde, though now it was a little darker, falling in soft waves around her face. Green eyes, so much like my own, shone above high cheekbones.

She lifted her hands, spreading them in front of her. "Geoffrey and I were in Orlando for a meeting last weekend. We fly back to California tonight, but I couldn't be that close and not stop to see you."

I shifted, uncomfortable. "You could've called me. I would've met you somewhere."

"Would you have, Abby? I didn't want to take the chance that you'd be too busy."

I felt the not-so-subtle rebuke and winced, remember how often I'd ignored texts or emails. "I'm sure we could've worked something out."

"Well, I'm here now. Do you have a minute for some coffee? Or maybe even breakfast?"

Beside me, Jude cleared her throat. I pasted a smile on my face. "Mom, this is Jude Holt. She owns this restaurant, and she and her husband Logan own the B&B and the hotel I'm going to be running." I cast Jude wide, pleading eyes. "Jude, this is my mother, Brooke Adams."

As the two of them exchanged hellos, I managed to get to my feet without falling. "Jude, is it okay if we go get some breakfast? I'll work later tonight."

She rolled her eyes. "Abby, don't be silly. Get a table over there, and I'll make whatever you want. Take your time and enjoy the visit with your mother."

Mom smiled. "Thank you, Jude. I appreciate it."

Jude winked. "I have a daughter, too. I know how much we miss them when they're grown up and on their own."

For the next half-hour, I ate eggs and made small talk with my mother, telling her about the history of the Riverside, what we'd done to restore the building, and the plans I had for her future.

"A spa! Well, isn't that a lovely idea. I'll have to book a weekend there. Oh, you know what? Jessica could come with me, and the three of us could have a mother-daughter pampering weekend!" Her eyes lit up at the thought.

I bit back the surge of resentment. I loved my little sister, or at least I loved her in theory. But it never failed to hurt me that our mother was so much more comfortable with Jess than she was with me.

"I'll have to see. Weekends will be difficult for me to get any free time." I took a fortifying sip of coffee. "I won't have a staff, like Daddy does. It'll be just me at first, plus some part-time employees, until we get everything up and running."

"I'm sure we can work it out." Mom smiled, which meant she wouldn't take no for an answer. I was about to change the subject when my phone buzzed with an incoming text message.

Where are you? Everything okay?

Ryland. Of course he'd be looking for me, since I'd started coming in early enough to see him before the crews arrived.

"Excuse me, Mom. I need to answer this." I tapped in a quick response and hit send.

Fine. I got a little held up but will be there within the hour.

I was being optimistic, hoping I could finish with my mother and be on the site by then. I felt her gaze on me.

"Sorry. I usually go in first thing each morning to talk

about what we're doing on the project. The con—uh, the restorations specialist was wondering where I am."

"Oh, sweetie! I'm so sorry. You should've said something." My mother pushed away her coffee cup and took a sip of water. "I don't want to hold you up from work." She looked disappointed for the space of a few breathes, and then she brightened. "Well, why can't I go over with you? I'm dying to see the place now that you've told me about it."

"Uhhh . . ." I tried to come up with a good, viable reason why my mother couldn't be there. But the idea well was empty. "I guess so. But you have to remember it's not finished yet. The walls aren't painted and of course, there's no furniture or window treatments."

Mom tilted her head. "Abby, you might remember, I've seen hotels in various states of construction and disrepair. When your father and I were first married, I was the one in charge of what you're doing now. I think I can handle it."

"All right, fine." I stood up and waved to Jude, who was chatting with her sister-in-law at the bar. "Can you just add breakfast to my tab, please?"

She shooed me away. "Don't be silly, it's on the house." With a broad grin, she added, "It was a treat to meet you, Mrs. Adams. Come back again soon."

My mother laughed, a bright tinkling sound that reminded me of my childhood. "Please, call me Brooke. Mrs. Adams makes me think I should be wearing a powdered wig and a bustle."

"Okay, come on, Mom." I stood by the door. "Do you want to follow me over? That way you could just leave from there, instead of having to drive back here."

"Why don't I ride with you? We can keep catching up."

I stifled a sigh. "Sure. My car's out here."

I expected more of the same meaningless chatter on the way to the hotel, but instead, my mother turned to face me. "Abby, one of the reasons I came up here was to talk with you about Jess."

My forehead wrinkled. "What's going on?"

"She's having some . . . issues. Geoffrey and I don't know what to do."

I snorted. "She's, what, twenty-six now? I'd think it isn't your problem anymore. She'll find herself."

But Mom only shook her head. "You don't know the background, Abby. Jessica . . . she's gone through some rough times." My mother gripped the handle of her purse. "She's been in and out of the hospital. We're so worried."

My mouth was dry. "Drugs?"

"No. She's never done anything like that, to my knowledge, anyway. It's better for her to tell you about it. Won't you come out and see her? She misses you, Abby. She needs her big sister."

I remembered the expression on Jessica's face the day I'd announced I was staying with Daddy. She'd been so hurt. We'd never been as close as other sisters, even before that day, but still, I loved her. I wondered if it were time to try to mend that fence.

"I'll call her." It was the most I could do right now. "I can't leave the Cove until after the hotel's up and running." An idea occurred to me, and I offered it. "She could come see me. Maybe it would be good for her—a change of scenery."

Mom clasped her hands together. "That might be exactly what she needs." She looked out the window at the passing scenery of the Cove as we made our way to the Riverside. "This little town is so pretty. I can see why you've settled here." She let the hint of a smile curve her lips. "Quite a nice change after Boston."

I didn't answer right away. I hadn't told my mother anything about what had happened in Boston; she hadn't even known about Zachary, unless of course my father had spilled the beans during one of his occasional late-night drunken phone calls to her. After I'd gotten settled here, the only reason I'd given Mom and Jess about my abrupt move was that I was tired of working for Dad. I knew that was something they'd both easily accept.

"Crystal Cove is a pretty amazing place. I love what I do, I've made some good friends . . . and it's mine, you know? I don't have to answer to anyone but Jude and Logan."

"I'm happy for you, Abby." She covered my hand where it gripped the steering wheel. "And I'm proud of you for making the right decision."

It was on the tip of my tongue to admit that I hadn't so much made the decision as been backed into a corner, but in the end, I just swallowed and forced a weak smile.

Mom was duly impressed as we drove onto the grounds of the hotel and parked the car. I led her down the same path I took every day, nerves dancing in my stomach as I wondered what she'd think of Ryland. My mother wasn't a snob by any means. On the other hand, I'd never introduced to her to any of my boyfriends, since they'd been so few and far between.

Of course, there was a good chance she'd never guess there was anything between us. Although Lincoln knew the truth, Ryland and I were careful to maintain a professional relationship in front of the crew. If I were honest, I'd admit it was kind of exciting to pretend we were still Mr. Kent and Ms. Donavan, all the while I knew that the minute we were alone in the hotel, Ryland would back me in a corner and kiss me until neither of us could think straight.

Each time he touched me, I knew I was closer to taking that last step with him. I still had a few Chinese food containers in my fridge, and when I saw them, the only thing I thought of was sharing steamed dumplings with him between the sheets. I didn't have a good reason for waiting anymore; I trusted Ryland, and there wasn't any doubt that I wanted him as much as he did me. At this point, it was only a matter of logistics and timing.

But I had to admit that the build-up and anticipation were the sweetest torture I'd ever known.

I sighed a little, and my mother cast me a curious side glance as we climbed the steps to the porch. I refocused on getting through her impromptu visit. Time enough later to think about jumping Ryland's bones.

"This is the main building, of course. Originally, this path from river was much wider, since most of the traffic came from that direction, and they used a little oxcart to transport luggage from the boats to the hotel."

"I can just imagine it." Mom turned in a circle, taking it all in. "It's so wonderful you're bringing her back to her glory days." She shook her head and gave me a small, self-deprecating smile. "I know it sounds silly, but whenever I see an old building like this come back to life, I think it must be happy, you know? It's so heart-breaking when something beautiful is left to fall into ruins, and such a kick to see it restored."

"Who are you, and where've you been all my life? I'm pretty sure I want to marry you."

I didn't have to turn around to recognize the voice coming from the doorway. Rolling my eyes, I turned to shoot Ryland what I hoped was a look of warning. "Mom, this is Ryland Kent, the restoration specialist overseeing the Riverside project. Mr. Kent, this is my mother, Brooke Adams."

Mom extended her hand, her eyes shining. "Of course I've heard of you, Mr. Kent. When we had some of the original buildings on my husband's vineyards rebuilt, Geoffrey looked into your company. Unfortunately, you were already booked for the timeframe we needed. We used Leo Groff, and he spoke very highly of you."

Ryland grinned. "Good old Leo. I started out working for him, many moons ago. Well, I'm sorry I couldn't fit in your project, Mrs. Adams. Even sorrier now that I've met you."

My mother's cheeks went pink, and I wanted to roll my eyes again. Apparently Ryland's ability to charm Donavan women knew no generational bounds.

"Please, call me Brooke. I have to say, my daughter didn't do you justice."

Ryland's eyes flew to mine, questioning, but if my mother noticed, she didn't give any indication as she went on.

"She said you're the best in the field and have enormous

talent, but this . . ." Mom spread her hands to encompass all of the hotel. "I saw the before pictures. You've worked a miracle."

Ryland chuckled. "Not done yet, but thanks. I think she's going to be absolutely gorgeous." I knew he was talking about the Riverside, but his gaze hadn't left my face. It felt as though I could feel it against my skin, like a physical caress.

"Will you show me around? Both of you?" Mom reached to take my hand. "I want to see it all."

And see it all she did. Sometimes I forgot how astute my mother was about—well, about everything. She'd been eighteen and studying interior design when she met my father, who'd just bought his first hotel. He hired her on the cheap, married her two months later, and together the two of them had built the Donavan Hotel brand. Even after their divorce, he still consulted with her on some aspects of design, although she no longer had any formal standing in the company. And she'd met Geoffrey when he'd hired her to handle the interior of new winery buildings.

We ran into Linc in one of the spa rooms. He and my mother immediately struck up a conversation about what we were doing in the buildings formerly known as the stables. The two of them were so absorbed that Ryland drifted into the hallway, motioning for me to follow.

"I'm sorry," I whispered. "I had no idea she was coming today. It was a surprise."

He took my hand, rubbing his thumb over the back of it. "Don't be sorry. Your mom is pretty terrific, and I'm glad I got to meet her." His eyes drifted down me, taking in the

172

short-sleeved fitted shirt and coordinating skirt. "You're beautiful every day, but damn, Abby. Those skirts. Are you trying to kill me?"

I pressed my back against the wall. "If my mother and Linc weren't in the other room, what would you be doing right now?"

Ryland growled low, just under his breath, and when he spoke, it was so quiet I had to strain to hear him. "I'd have my body up against yours, and those perfect tits in my hands. I'd be ravishing your lips, kissing you until you had to beg me for your next breath. And I'd be grinding my—"

"Well, this has been just wonderful." My mother's voice rang out from within, and I heard the click of her heels approaching. "Abby? Are you out here?" She poked her head around the edge of the door. "Oh, there you are. I'm sorry, were Lincoln and I boring you two? I'm sure you're tired of hearing the same old stuff over and over."

I cleared my throat, hoping she couldn't hear the pounding of my heart or feel the need pulsing off my body. I didn't dare look at Ryland, for fear I'd just go up in flames right then and there.

"Um, no, not bored. I just needed to go over a few things for today with Mr. Kent." I deliberately used the name that I knew drove him wild, and as I said it, I toyed with the hem of my skirt, hoping he was watching. "Are you ready, Mom? If your flight leaves from Orlando at three, you probably need to get back down to the airport."

"Sadly, that's true. But now that I've been here and seen the Riverside, I'm afraid you won't be able to keep me away. I'll have to bring Geoffrey out for a weekend once it's open."

She beamed at me. "I can see your hand all over this place, Abby. You—and these gentlemen, of course—have done this old hotel proud."

I felt a surge of gladness at her affirmation. I hadn't realized how much I wanted my mother to approve of my life now—of my work, of where I lived. It was more important than I'd known.

After she'd hugged both Linc and Ryland good-bye— yes, my mother was a hugger, although clearly that gene had skipped me in the generational gambit—we walked back up the path to my car. I'd just turned the key in the ignition when she laid a hand on my arm.

"Abby, I was serious when I said I'm proud of you." She hesitated for a beat, and I sensed she was trying to find the right words. "After Boston, I felt so helpless. There wasn't anything I could do to make it better, to help you. So when the information about the bed and breakfast fell into my lap, I'm afraid I acted impulsively, and afterwards, I wondered if I'd done the right thing or if I'd been motivated by a subconscious, selfish desire to get you away from Colin."

My head spun, and I frowned, trying to follow the lines of what my mother was saying. "Wait a minute. You knew— how did you know about Boston?"

Mom's forehead drew together. "Well, first I heard about it from Jana, and then again from Corrine. Did you think they wouldn't mention it to me?"

I bit down on my bottom lip, trying to make sense of her words. "Daddy's secretary Jana? And Auntie Corrine? I didn't even know you were in touch with either of them."

"Abby." There was more than subtle reproach in my

mother's voice. "Did you really think I'd let my daughter go off with a man like Colin—yes, even if he is your father— without having a plan in place to watch over things? Jana's been keeping her eye on you for years. Since I left, in San Francisco. And Corrine and I have always been friends. I'm grateful you have someone like her in your life, if it can't be me."

Tears rose in my eyes, and I couldn't stop them from rolling down my face. "I didn't think you wanted me. After—after what I did. Staying with Daddy. The way I treated you."

"Abby. Baby." She cupped my cheek in her hand. "I never blamed you for that. You were a child, and you made that decision based on information you had and loyalty to your father, neither of which was your fault. I was hurt, and I was sad, but I was never angry. And I hoped, once you were older and could see things a little more clearly, that we might . . . mend fences. Be close again."

I closed my eyes and leaned my head back. "After I found out about what Daddy was really doing, I was too ashamed to go back to you. And by then you had Geoffrey, and you and Jess were making a new life with him. It felt like that didn't include me."

"There was always room for you, Abby. You just had to claim it." Mom sighed. "You have a double dose of the stubborn, you know, from both me and your dad. It took me years of misery before I left him—not because I was afraid or still so in love with him, but because of my pride. Everyone had told me I was fool for marrying this brash kid when I was only eighteen, and I wanted to prove them wrong. That's why I stayed so long. And then one day I realized all I had was pride—and you girls. The pride was cold company, and the last thing I wanted you both to have as your example of married life was what I had with your father. That's why I finally left."

"And that's why I didn't tell you about Boston." I wiped at my cheeks. "I'd made the choice to stay with Daddy, to work for him, and I wanted to prove that I could make a go of it." I paused as some of my mother's words filtered into my brain. "You said something about information on the bed and breakfast falling into your lap—what does that mean? Did you have something to do with me getting the job at the Hawthorne House?"

A slightly guilty expression crept over Mom's face. "I thought you knew. Yes, the woman who runs the B&B down the road from us in Napa—I think you've met her—had been out here on vacation, and she mentioned that she'd been talking to people in Crystal Cove who were going to open their own place. She said they were looking for a reliable manager, and since she's in the business, she was trying to help them out. I'd just heard about everything that happened to you in Boston, so I made the call. I talked to a man who said his business partner had recently passed away, and he and the man's widow were going ahead with plans to open the B&B. I said that I knew of a very responsible, reliable manager who was currently looking for a new opportunity, and I gave him your name and email."

It all made sense now. I'd thought ending up in the Cove had been a fluke, just something that had happened to me. But all the time, my mother had been keeping an eye on me.

I wondered if I should resent that fact, but I didn't. Instead, I felt . . . loved. Cherished, in a way I hadn't experienced for a very long time.

"I wondered if interfering was a mistake, but it seems as though you're happy here." She twisted the strap of her purse between her fingers, and I realized she was nervous.

"I am, Mom." I covered her fidgeting fingers with my own hand, stilling the movement. "The Cove is home. I can't imagine living anywhere else. I'm happier here than I've ever been. So thank you. I never guessed you were the reason I'm here, but I'm grateful. I have a job I love, good friends and a brand new hotel to live in, eventually."

"And Ryland?" A note of wiliness crept into my mother's tone. "He's making you happy, too?"

I blew out a breath. "How did you figure that out?"

She laughed. "Because I'm your mother. And he looks at you like you're the dessert in four-course meal. Like you're the most incredible person he's ever met." She nudged me. "Which of course you are. But you didn't answer me. Does he make you happy?"

I struggled to put what I felt for Ryland into words. Words that were suitable for my mother's ears, that is. "It's new between us. We clashed from the minute we met, we fought and we argued . . . until we didn't. But I think . . . I think it's good. He makes me feel beautiful and special—and I can trust him. I can be Abby with him, not just Abigail Donavan."

"I'm so glad for you, honey." My mother sniffed and dabbed at her eyes. "If that's the case, if this man makes you glow like I've seen—hold onto him. Don't let stubbornness or pride get in the way. The chance for happiness doesn't come strolling down the road every day. When it does, you have to grab it before it passes you by."

I grinned. "I think I might do just that."

chapter eleven

Ryland

"ALL THE PAINT SHOULD BE delivered by the middle of next week, and we'll have the main building finished in about ten, eleven days. Two weeks, tops."

I leaned into the railing on the porch, looking over the lawn. "Landscaping is set to get underway about that time, too."

"Yep. We're officially on the homestretch now." Linc stood, twisting his upper body as he groaned. "Isn't this about the time you take off to find the next one?"

I'd known this was coming. I shrugged, not meeting his eyes. "Nothing on the horizon yet. We're rolling into the slow time of year, so it's not surprising. And you know how

I feel about this project. I'm sticking with it to the end."

"How you feel about this project, or how you feel about the lady boss?" Linc smirked. "The one whose bones you were about to jump this afternoon while I was chatting up her mom? We walked out and it felt like I was swimming in—what's the stuff that attracts us to other people? The crap we smell, but we don't know we're smelling it? Oh, yeah, pheromones. It was thick, man. You going to get busy with her, or just keep stringing each other along?"

I gritted my teeth. "We're just taking things slow, Linc. It's not always about the wham and the bam, you know. Sometimes a little lead-up time makes everything . . . better."

He held up his hands. "Preaching to the choir, buddy. You didn't know me then, but when Sylvia and I first got together, she kept me on the hooks for months." He smiled a little, remembering, and I realized it was the first time he'd talked about her without the look of pain I'd gotten used to seeing whenever her name came up. If this was a sign of healing, I was glad.

"Then why're you yanking my chain about Abby?" I rested my hands on my hips.

"Because it's never been your style. You're usually all about the in and out, excuse my imagery." He winked. "I've never known you to play along with the hard-to-get game."

"Maybe no other girl's ever been worth playing." My phone buzzed, and I pulled it out of my pocket. When I saw the text was from Abby, I felt the sappy smile curl up my lips.

Are you free tonight? It's my turn to take you on a date.

Anticipation sizzled through me. I hadn't been lying to

Linc—or to myself—about my slow build-up, but damn, I was ready to move to the next level. Primed and ready.

Sounds like an offer I don't want to refuse. Where and when, sexy?

"Hey, you listening to me?" Linc's voice intruded on my happy place. "Or are you going to stand there mooning over whatever the lady boss just told you?"

"Uhh, did you say something?"

Linc released a sigh of exasperation. "Yeah, I did. I said, you're wrong about there not being any jobs in the pipe. I got a call about a gig in St. Louis."

"Uh huh." The phone buzzed again. I couldn't not look.

Tonight. Seven o'clock. Meet me on the beach in front of the Tide. Comfortable clothes.

I raised my eyebrows. The beach, huh? That sounded intriguing. Evenings were getting a little chilly this time of year, but nothing a sweatshirt wouldn't solve. Before I could type an answer, she sent a follow-up text.

Oh, and Ryland? Tell Linc you won't be home tonight.

Hot damn. Tonight was the night, and God, I was so onboard with that, it was ridiculous.

"Of course, usually St. Louis in December would be a little tricky, but apparently this is a unique situation. It's all interior work they need. Some other company did all the structural stuff, everything on the outside, before they went bankrupt. The owners are in a panic, needing someone to come in and finish up the inside." Linc crossed his arms over his chest. "Sounds like something just up your alley, huh?"

I couldn't think about this right now. The idea of leaving the Cove made my stomach clench, and I wasn't stupid; I knew it wasn't the job or the weather. It was Abby. It blew my mind that the woman who'd irritated the living hell out of me had become one of the most important people in my life—and we hadn't even slept together yet.

"I'll think about it." It was the most I could give Linc at this point. "We'll talk later, okay? Right now . . . I'm going home to grab a shower. I've got a date tonight. Oh, and Linc, buddy?" I grinned at him as I jumped from the porch to the ground. "Don't wait up."

The sun was just beginning to set when I parked my truck in the empty lot next to the Riptide and headed down the path that led to the beach. During the week, the Tide closed at five, and everything was quiet. I could hear the pounding of the surf against the sand as I came up over the dunes.

Just beyond the small hills, Abby sat on a blanket. Her back was to me, and her jet black hair blew in the cool wind. She was leaning on her arms with her legs out in front, fac-ing the waves. A square wicker basket was next to her, and I spotted a bottle of wine, too.

Whether she heard my footsteps or just sensed me, I didn't know, but she turned, her big green eyes seeking me out. A long-sleeved cotton shirt clung to her chest, remind-ing me of the small firm breasts beneath, and a long skirt was tucked under her legs. When I caught the expression on her face, the warm gladness at seeing me and the promise of what was to come, I couldn't get to her fast enough.

She sat waiting for me, tracking my approach. I dropped onto the blanket next to her, my hip bumping up against hers. "Hi."

It was lame, but it was all I could manage. Somehow seeing her here, perfect and beautiful and so god-damned desirable, had robbed me of any coherent thought.

"Hi, Ryland." She turned then, shifting toward me as she curled her legs under the cloth of her skirt, wrapping it around her feet. "I'm glad you're here." She lifted up just a little, leaning into me as she touched her lips to mine. It was a light kiss, gentle and tentative, but it broke something inside me. I held her face, deepening the connection and pouring into her all the want and all the need churning within me. When I released her, it was only to lean my forehead into hers.

"There's no place else in the world I'd rather be."

She smiled, sitting back. "I have food, too." Opening the basket, she glanced at me over her shoulder. "Not Chinese food, but I think you'll like it." Pulling out several different wrapped packets, she began to peel back the foil. "Fried chicken. Potato salad. Biscuits." She reached back into the hamper and brought out two glasses. "And a really excellent Pinot Grigio I liberated from behind the bar at the Tide."

I raised my eyebrows. "Why, Abigail Donavan, did you steal this wine?"

She laughed. "Not really. I got permission from Jude, and I left a note for it to go on my tab."

"Damn. Here I thought I'd really corrupted you."

She tilted her head. "Not yet. Give it time."

Oh, baby.

Abby made us each a plate, and I virtually inhaled the food. "God, Abby, this is delicious. Did you make it?"

She smiled. "I did. After Mom left today, I took the rest of the afternoon off, went shopping for all the ingredients, and started cooking." She wiped her lips with a napkin. "My kitchen was too small, so I sweet-talked Jude into letting me use the one in the Tide. It's so much easier to make fried chicken in a deep fryer."

"I wouldn't know from personal experience, but if this is the result, yeah, I'd have to agree. It's amazing. And I've never tasted biscuits so good. Where'd you learn to cook, Abby?"

She leaned against me, the warmth of her body seeping into my bones. "Lots of places. I made my first fried chicken and biscuits when we lived at the hotel in Atlanta. The head cook there was very patient with me. The potato salad I picked up in Indianapolis. One of the sous chefs had been in the army, and he used to make this stuff by the gallon."

"So living all over the country had some benefits, huh?" I snagged another drumstick and bit into it.

"Oh, I always loved it. I used to be so excited when we were about to close the deal on a new property in a new city." She lifted one shoulder. "Until I got older. And then it got a little wearying."

"Did you ever think about moving in with your mom?"

She shook her head. "Not really. I knew it was always an option, I guess, but by then, I looked at each new hotel as more on-the-job training for me."

"How did things go today? With your mother, I mean."

I expected her to tense up a little, but instead, Abby let

out a long breath, her face relaxing into a beautiful smile. "It was . . . amazing. So much better than I could've ever thought. I mean, at first I was annoyed when she just showed up, but by the end, we really talked." She snuggled closer to me as the wind picked up. "My mom is the one who got me the job at the Hawthorne House. She knew about Boston and Zachary all along."

I finished the chicken and tossed the bone onto my empty plate. "You were okay with that?"

"More than. Turns out I like the idea of having a mom who cares enough to interfere in my life." Abby rested her head against my shoulder. "She liked you."

I smirked. "And you're surprised? What's not to like? I'm a great catch, Donavan. I own my own company. I'm a hard worker. I'm healthy, with no seriously bad habits. And I'm damned sexy."

The corners of her lips tipped up. "Yes, you are." With a small contented sigh, she looked out over the ocean as she finished her last piece of chicken and licked some crumbs from her fingers.

Watching her small pink tongue dart out to touch her finger made it suddenly hard to swallow. I captured her hand and brought it to my own mouth. "Let me." With agonizing slowness, I drew one of her fingers between my lips, sucking on it before I swirled my tongue over the salty skin as all the blood in my body surged southward. I couldn't remember ever wanting a woman the way I needed this one right now.

Abby's breath hitched, but her eyes never left mine. They dilated until there was almost more black than green, and her lips parted. "Ryland . . . "

I paused, raising one eyebrow, her finger still in my mouth.

"Let's go upstairs. To my apartment. I don't want to wait anymore."

We tossed both food and trash back into the basket in record time. I carried it and the blanket, while Abby handled the wine bottle and our glasses. We didn't speak much as we trudged toward the Riptide, through the empty restaurant and up the stairs to Abby's place. The door was unlocked, and I held it open for her before I followed her inside and dropped the basket on the small kitchen floor.

Abby set down the wine bottle, draining her glass before she put it on the table, too. When she turned to look up at me, the control I'd been hanging onto with the thinnest of threads snapped.

I grabbed her by the waist and walked her backwards until she bumped into her bedroom door. When we couldn't move any further, I bent to ravish her mouth—no slow build up here; I took her, aggressively consuming each breath and each small incoherent noise she made. My tongue swept through her mouth, and hers tangled with it, thrusting forward to stroke before it pulled back to tease.

"Ryland . . ." Abby moaned my name, and I thought I'd never heard anything so beautiful. My dick swelled under the zipper of my jeans, and I needed more of her, now. I needed my lips to be all over her. I wanted to taste and to touch every part of her intoxicating body.

Lifting her by the hips, I brought her face level to mine and tore my mouth away from her lips, nibbling down the line of her jaw to the slim white column of her neck. When I reached her delicate collarbone, I moved my hand to grip her upper thigh.

"Wrap your legs around me." I didn't have it in me to add please or to make it a request; need had taken over, and now nothing else existed. It pounded a rhythm that was impossible not to follow.

Abby tried to lift her legs and groaned in frustration. "I can't—my skirt is caught."

I leaned over, still pinning her body to the door, and jerked the material upwards, freeing her limbs. She twined her legs around me, aligning my aching cock with the center of her own desire. I slid my hands up to her ribs and then over her boobs, relishing the moan that tore from her lips. Tugging down the neckline of her shirt, I fumbled to hook my fingers under the cup of her bra.

When I managed it, the back of my hand skimmed over her nipple so that it hardened into a stiff point. I pulled down again, exposing more of her, and palmed her breast, holding the soft fullness within my grasp. The tension of her bra pushed her boob upward, presenting the tempting peak.

"Ryland—yes. Please, yes." Abby was begging, panting, as I lowered my mouth to the enticing pink tip. Another time, I might have teased and made her wait. But tonight, now, I didn't have it in me. I fastened my lips there and sucked, hard, my tongue pressing her nipple against the roof of my mouth, until her hips ground into me restlessly.

Releasing it from my mouth, I kept my hand on one tit, rubbing the nipple between two fingers, while I moved my mouth to the other side. I dropped my free hand to grip her firm ass. With the material of her skirt hiked around her waist, only a thin layer of silk panties was between me and the smooth skin. I stroked her, each time letting my touch stray a tiny bit closer to the part of her body that I wanted most.

I released her nipple to murmur in her ear. "Do you want me to touch you, Abby? Want my fingers to slide over you, press against your clit, slip them inside you and stroke until you shatter around me? Is that what you want?"

"Yesssss." The word was a moan, wrenched from her lips, and I didn't hesitate. I slid my fingers beneath her underwear, groaning when I felt the wet heat of her pussy. She tilted just a little, in an effort to make me touch her where she needed me. I didn't make her wait any longer; I found the pulsing button of nerves and pressed hard as she arched into my hand.

Before she could fall over the edge, I plunged two fingers inside her tight channel, rubbing her clit with my thumb, relentless and with increasing speed until she screamed, her hips undulating of their own accord as her hands clutched at my shoulders.

I brought her down slowly, stroking, murmuring soft nonsensical words into her ear. Abby slumped against me, her head falling to rest on my chest. "Ryland . . . my God. I've never . . . wow. Just wow."

I kissed the top of her head. "Right there with you, babe." My voice was a little strained; watching her come had only made me harder, made me want her all the more.

"Can we go into the bedroom now?" She stroked one hand down my chest and over my stomach, bringing it to rest on the straining denim between my legs. "I might be able to think of something else you'd enjoy. One or two ideas seem to have . . . sprung to mind."

I clenched my jaw. She was killing me. Who knew under that cool exterior, this chick burned so freaking hot? "I think I can manage that." I scooped Abby into my arms, turned the doorknob and pushed into her bedroom.

The room was like the woman herself: neat, comfortable, stylish without being flashy. A large bed, covered with a cotton quilt in muted colors, dominated the space. I lay Abby down there and toed off my shoes before joining her.

She pushed up onto her elbows, smiling down at me. "So this is my bedroom."

I grinned back. "I like it. But I have to say, I would've pegged you to have one of those fancy shiny bedspreads. This is nice."

Abby giggled. "I can't stand any silky or satiny bedding. It's too slippery. Everything falls off and it drives me crazy."

"Practical. I like that."

"Hmmm." She sat up and crossed her legs. "The practical side of me says we both have too many clothes still on."

"Really?" I pretended to think about it. "You know, you might be right. What're we going to do about that?"

"I'll start here." She reached for the hem of her shirt and pulled it off over her head. But when she moved her hands to the waistband of her skirt, I stayed them with my own.

"No. Leave that." I trailed my hand over the smooth

skin of her stomach. "I want to be inside you, with your skirt on and ruched up around your waist. Just take off your bra. And your panties."

Abby's eyes went molten again, and her tongue came out to touch her bottom lip. She didn't say anything, just reached back to release the hook on her bra. I groaned when her breasts spilled out, free.

"God, Abby, you're so fucking gorgeous." I touched one nipple with the tip of my finger, all the blood rushing to my already-engorged dick when Abby sucked in a breath on a hiss. "Do you have any idea what you do to me? You just . . . consume me. All I can think about is you, touching you, kissing you—talking with you, arguing with you, holding you. Wanting to be inside you. God, Abby, I want that more than anything else in the world."

She rose up on her knees, lifting her skirt and reaching beneath to wriggle out of her underwear. Tossing it off the mattress, she turned back to me with a smile that turned me inside out. One small hand pushed me flat on the bed.

"Mr. Kent, I think I can make that happen." With one fluid movement, she straddled me, tugging my shirt from the waistband of my jeans. Her hands were warm as she slid them against my stomach and chest, taking my shirt with her. I helped her get it over my head, and then it was gone, too, flying onto the floor to join her clothes.

Abby bent over me, raining small kisses over my chest, pausing to circle my nipples with her tongue.

"Baby, that feels amazing." I smoothed one hand down her back, stroking her hair. "Your mouth on me is fucking incredible."

"Think so? Well, Mr. Kent, let's see how you feel about this."

She unbuttoned my jeans and pulled down the zipper, humming in what I sincerely hoped was appreciation when my erection sprang free from the boxers under my jeans. I lifted my hips so that she could get the pants off me.

And then there she was, her head between my legs, looking up at me with speculation. I watched in utter fascination as she held my cock at the base and with slowness I thought might truly be the death of me, lowered her mouth to take me inside.

I was in heaven. There wasn't any other explanation. The tight heat of her lips, firm around my dick, threatened to unhinge me. She took me in, bit by bit, until she couldn't move anymore, and then she lazily pulled back, scraping her teeth lightly over the hyper-sensitive skin. Her tongue circled the head, and just before she released me, she sucked once, hard. She repeated it all, this time with more intensity, moving faster and groaning so that the vibration of her voice hummed over my throbbing cock.

I was close, so close to losing control. When she slid her mouth over me again, I touched the back of her head.

"Abby—babe—I'm going to—I want to be inside you. When I come. You're killing me right now."

She lifted her eyes to look at me. "Is that a good thing?"

I managed a strangled laugh. "Oh, it's peaches, baby, but I've been fantasizing about coming inside you for so long, I don't want to wait anymore. Let me get something out of my jeans."

She crawled back up my body. "Do you mean a condom? I have some in my drawer here."

I laid down again, surprised. "You do? I thought didn't—you hadn't been with anyone. Since you've been in the Cove, I mean."

"I haven't. I bought them today, right after I texted you." She sounded so self-assured, so completely Abigail Donavan, that I couldn't help shaking my head.

"Abby, you're the most amazing woman I've ever met."

She frowned. "Why? Because I bought condoms?"

"No." I shook my head. "Because it just doesn't seem like what I'd expect from you. At work you come off as so in charge, so controlled. Like sex, like this, would be the last thing on your mind. And yet, tonight, with me . . . you're a wild woman. In the best way possible. And the fact that you went out today and bought condoms turns me on even more, because it means you were thinking about tonight, too. Just like I was."

Abby leaned over to open a drawer and came back to sit next to me. "I'm not that experienced, not with sex. But I do a lot of reading." She tore open the package with her teeth and took me in her hands again. Licking her lips, she rolled the rubber over me, each touch of her fingers setting me on fire.

I rolled her over beneath me, taking in the image of her laying on the white sheets, her black hair spread like silk, her eyes eager and her body reaching for mine. Kissing down her neck, I circled my tongue around one turgid nipple before settling myself between her legs. I held my cock, rubbing it up and down her swollen folds until she was writhing again, gasping. Begging.

I found her entrance and pushed in slowly, giving us both time to acclimate. Abby's fingers gripped my ass, urging me forward, and when she tilted her hips, I was lost. I thrust forward, seating myself within her so deep that at first I feared I'd hurt her when she cried out.

But she was only wanting more, and that I could do. I pulled out and then stroked back inside her, each movement deliberate and harder. I was barely holding myself back when I felt her begin to pulse around my dick. It was the end of me; with a deep growl, I pounded myself into her, plunging both of us into oblivion as pleasure poured into our bodies.

I fell panting onto the mattress, pulling her to lay on top of me so that I didn't crush her slim body. My heart was pounding, and I was sure she could hear it. Her fingers skimmed up to cover that part of my chest, and she lifted her head just enough to press a kiss there.

"Abby . . ." I smoothed my hand down her back, over her hair, letting it come to rest on the firm rise of her backside. "Oh, baby. You just . . . you blow my mind."

I felt the curve of her smile against me. "Right back at you, Mr. Kent."

I breathed out a laugh. "Watch it, woman. I'm done in now, but give me a few minutes, and *Mr. Kent* will take you again."

She giggled. "Did it really drive you crazy when I'd call you that, and not your first name? I mean, before."

I rubbed her back. "It did, mostly because I felt like it was your way of keeping me at arms' length. And that was okay, until that day when it stormed, and I knew. I knew I wanted you, but you still shut me out. Then I thought you were only calling me that to protect yourself from me."

Abby sighed, her soft breath raising goose bumps on me. "From now on, when I call you Mr. Kent, it'll just be my signal that I'm thinking of . . ." Her hand danced down to touch me lower, just below my navel. "All business. Of a very special sort."

"That's a deal, Abby." My eyes began to drift close.

She snuggled closer. "I like that you call me Abby." Her voice slurred with drowsiness. "Zachary always called me Abigail. He said Abby sounded too informal and silly. That irritated the hell out of me."

I turned a little, pulling her closer and tucking her head beneath my chin. "Zachary was a dick. I'm glad he never called you that. You're *my* Abby, for always."

That thought spread over me, warm and comforting, as we both slid into sleep.

chapter twelve

Abby

"**M**y God, woman, you're going to kill me." My head emerged from beneath the sheet, a sleepy smile spread over my mouth. "I hope not. You're not any good to me dead."

Ryland laughed, threading his fingers into my hair to sweep it away from my eyes. "Good morning, by the way. That's about the nicest way I've woken up in . . . ever."

I stretched, languorous as a cat in the sunshine. "It only seemed right, after you returned the favor, oh, five times last night."

"True. You did keep me up most of the night. My boss is going to pissed when I fall asleep on the job."

It was very early, and the sun was only a soft glow on

the ocean. It was a weekday, which meant we both had to be on the job site in an hour or two. But for now, we were in my bed, entwined in each other.

"My alarm's going to go off in a few minutes." I nuzzled Ryland's neck. "Do you have to go back to Cooper's to get ready for work?"

His eyes stayed closed, but he smiled. "Someone might have thought ahead and left a change of clothes in the front seat of his truck. So if someone else will let me use her shower, I can leave from here." He opened one eye. "That is, if you don't mind that Jude might see me coming down from your apartment."

I shook my head. "That cat's out of the bag. She figured it out yesterday, before my mom got here. Let me tell you, keeping a secret in this town's a piece of work."

"True enough." Whatever he might have said next was lost as music erupted from my phone. I scrambled to turn it off.

"Sorry. I have to keep it turned up loud or I'll sleep right through it. I'm not usually a morning person."

Ryland waggled his eyebrows at me. "Could've fooled me." He pushed to sit up, stuffing the pillow behind his back. "What was that song, anyway?"

Trepidation seized me. "Ummm . . . I don't know. Just a random song the phone picked, I guess."

"Bullshit. You have to program your phone to play music for the alarm." His eyes narrowed. "Abby, let me see your phone."

Crap. "No."

"Abby Donavan, give me your phone. It's better I find

out now than later."

I grabbed the phone from the nightstand and buried it under a pillow. "No."

"Abby." Ryland spoke with patient exasperation. "Give it here." When I didn't respond, he added, "Or I'll have to get it my way."

His fingers darted to my ribs, tickling, and then around to my stomach. I shrieked and gasped, trying to roll away, desperate to keep the phone out of his hands.

But it was a battle I lost. He wrested it from my grip and scooted away from me, sitting up against the headboard as he hit buttons and began to scroll. "Oh, my God. Oh, Abby. It's worse than I thought."

I burrowed my head into a pillow.

"Abby . . . the Carpenters? Helen Reddy? *Barry Manilow?*" He groaned. "Abby, say it isn't so. Tell me this isn't true." He clutched at his heart. "Tell me you're not a fan of . . . *easy listening* music?"

I sat up and crossed my arms over my chest, pushing out my bottom lip. "Okay. So I like that kind of music. What's wrong with that?"

"So much that I don't even know where to begin. Oh, wait, here's some redemption. The Beatles. Okay, you might not be too far gone. I might be able to save you."

I snorted. "Save me, huh?" I rescued my phone. "Maybe I don't want saving. Maybe I like me the way I am."

Ryland crawled over to me and kissed my lips. "I like you the way you are, too. I just want to help you improve your taste in music."

I blew out a sigh. "I can't help it. It's a sentimental fa-

197

vorite. When I was growing up, that was the kind of music that played in our hotels. And my mom loves the Carpenters, so when I hear them, it reminds me of a very happy part of my life."

He nodded, laying his head down on my stomach. "I understand that. But it doesn't mean you can't learn to appreciate other music. Dare I say it, even better music." When I started to protest, he put one finger to my lips. "Let's start here. What's your favorite Beatles song?"

I dropped my head back to the pillow. "*In My Life*. I love the lyrics. It just . . . it's important to me. It talks about places changing, and . . . love remaining the same. Of loving someone *more*. I always thought that was what made a true love. You know? My dad loves me, but he loves booze more. Zachary said he loved me, but he loved his career more. I wanted someone who loved me . . . more."

Ryland turned his head and looked up at me. His eyes were serious, thoughtful. He skimmed the back of his fingers over my cheek. "I know what you mean. It's my favorite, too, actually." He took the phone back from me, scrolled again and when it began to play the familiar opening chords of the song, he lay it on my chest, between his face and mine.

We stayed that way, unmoving, as the sun shot its opening beams across the bed, beginning a new day.

"I can't believe how quickly everything came together for the spa." I glanced around the wide foyer. "Hard to believe this used to house horses, huh?"

Ryland shook his head. "Let's not raise a sensitive topic."

I grinned. "Oh, come on. You have to admit that this place is beautiful. And a lot more useful than stables would've been in the twenty-first century."

He gave me a little nod. "Okay, I guess I can concede that much. And just think, you can play all your easy listening favorites in here to your heart's content, and no one's going to complain."

I shot him a nasty gesture, but he only laughed at me.

If I had known how much fun it could be to work with the same man who was in my bed every night, I might not have waited so long to make it happen. For the first week after Ryland and I began sleeping together, I'd waited for the other shoe to fall. I'd waited for the bad to follow the good. But when everything between us only continued to get better—both in bed and on the job site—I let myself relax and believe I might actually be able to make this work.

"Did you send the promotional stuff out for the grand opening?" Ryland stooped down to examine the underside of a window sill.

"Yes, everything's falling into place. There's a lot of excitement. We're going to have a television crew from the evening news covering it, and one of the radio stations is going to broadcast from here that afternoon. I got some face painters to come in, a few musicians . . . it's going to be like a carnival atmosphere."

A breeze blew over my skin, carrying as it often did the scent of lilacs. I'd had the sense that she was pleased, whatever or whoever it was still residing in these walls. I felt a banked excitement lately, as though she were just waiting to see the final result, as we all were.

"It's going to be amazing, because you're amazing." Ryland stood again, laced his fingers with me and drew me to him. "You should be proud of yourself, Abby. The River-side is going to shine again, and it's all because of you."

I smiled against his lips, opening my mouth and tangling my tongue with his. "I might've had a little help here and there."

"Yeah. You might've." He gave me one more fast kiss and then swatted my bottom. "Okay, woman. I have to get back to work. The paint should be finished in the main building today, and I want to make sure it's perfect before you see the final result."

Ryland had insisted that I stay out of the hotel proper while the final work was taking place. He wanted me to see it as a finished product, in its totality, and he was so excited about the idea that I'd agreed. I stuck to monitoring progress in the outbuildings, teasing him to give me just a small peek.

"All right. Get to work. I'm going to talk to the land-scapers for a few minutes about the shrubs around this building, and then I'm heading back to the office for the rest of the day." I smiled at Ryland. "Are we meeting at the Tide for dinner tonight?"

He grinned at me in return. "I thought we were having leftover Chinese. In bed. As a matter of fact, I think that was my fortune the other night. 'You will eat the rest of the copious amounts of food your woman ordered . . . in bed.'"

I laughed. "Okay, okay. It's a date. I'll be back at the

apartment after five."

"I'll be there around the same time."

I stood for a minute, watching through the window as Ryland strode across the lawn to the front of the hotel. A sense of something that might've been contentment stole over me, and I hugged my arms around my middle, simply soaking it in. For the first time that I could remember, my life felt . . . balanced. Right. Filled with easy affection, work I loved and a man who set my nights on fire. I hadn't admitted I was in love with Ryland, not yet, not even to myself. But if I were going to be honest, I knew it was true. He'd stolen my heart and crept into my soul.

I trusted him, more than I ever thought I could any man. But even so, a niggle of worry was buried in my heart. As much as I was anticipating the opening of the Riverside, part of me dreaded what came after. Ryland and I didn't talk about the future beyond that day. He hadn't mentioned moving or taking a new job, but neither had he made any plans that I knew of to stay here in the Cove. Taking everything a day at a time wasn't easy, but it was how I had to live right now.

And with days that began and ended in bed with Ryland Kent, I really couldn't complain.

"Abigail?"

The familiar voice intruded into my happy place, bringing the walls crashing down. I turned my head slowly, willing my ears to be wrong.

But they weren't. Zachary Todd stood in the doorway of the spa. He hadn't changed much in three years; maybe he was a bit heavier, his face a tad fuller. But the slightly mocking expression in his eyes, the pout of his lips and the affected way he had of moving . . . it was all there in force as he looked at me, speculation and smugness in his eyes.

"What the hell are you doing here?" I kept my voice low and steady. The key to Zachary, I'd learned from painful experience, was not letting him see any emotion or weakness. I stiffened my back and schooled my face to show nothing. "This is private property. It's also an active worksite. You're not permitted to be here."

"Oh, come on, Abigail. Don't be silly. I went to your office, and the secretary there told me that you were on the project site. I told her we were old friends, and I'd wanted to talk with you about the restaurant job here. She thought it would be fine for me stop by."

"She was wrong. And so were you, incidentally. We're not old friends, and the position here is filled. You weren't even in the running."

"Now that's a shame, since I'm clearly the most qualified candidate. I've been trying to call, to remind you of that fact. But my calls are never returned. Even so, I know I'm the right man for this position."

"How would you know that? You don't know who applied."

"I don't have to know. I know that I have more experience than anyone else, added to the fact that I've been running successful hotel-affiliated restaurants for ten years."

I barked a mirthless laugh. "That's open to interpretation. Tell me, how did you get your current job? I know you didn't have a reference from my father or anyone else at Donavan Hotels."

He smiled, and the sight of it sent a chill down my spine. "I have ways. I know people, and I have connections. And I'm very good at what I do."

"Maybe." He wasn't lying, but I didn't have to concede to anything. "But the fact of the matter remains. You're not getting the job here. I am curious, though. Why did you apply for this job? And were you really ballsy enough to think I'd give it to you, after everything that happened in Boston?"

Zachary leaned against the doorway, his casual ease effortless. "I know you, Abigail. You're like me. We understand that business is business, and there's no doubt that hiring me would be good business. It would send this backwater hotel into the stratosphere, put your name on the map." He paused. "As for why I'd want it, I would think that'd be clear. You may be hiding out down here in Florida, but you're a Donavan. One day, you'll return to the fold. You'll run Donavan Hotels. One day you'll *be* Donavan Hotels. When that happens, I want to be the one by your side, helping you to make it happen. It makes sense. Business sense."

My mouth sagged open. "Seriously? You think I'm that much of a pathetic idiot that I'd open myself up to you again? After what you did to me?"

He shook his head. "What happened between us in Boston was necessary so that you understood how important it is to separate business from emotion. You were young and naïve, Abigail. Now you know. We don't have to like each other to make this work. We're both cut from the same cloth: we don't need the attachment of a messy romantic affair. We're above all that."

"You'd be wrong about that, on all counts." The shock of seeing Zachary had worn away, and the mad I'd once told Emmy I'd never experienced? It was here now, in full force. And Zachary Todd was about to feel it.

"You'd be wrong about that all around. First of all, I have no plans to go back to Donavan Hotels. This is my home, and I plan to make the Riverside both a raving success and my permanent home. My last name may be Donavan, but that's not my life. Second, I'm nothing like you. Nothing. I don't treat people like resources. I don't look at life as though it's all business. I'm a passionate woman, Zachary. I burn hot. You never knew that, of course, because you're not man enough to ignite me."

He flinched, and I knew I'd hit a nerve.

"It would be a cold, cold day in hell before I'd hire you for anything, let alone trust you with the restaurant here. Be happy with the little niche you've managed to carve out in Tennessee, because it's as far as you get. If you try anything else, if you mess with Donavan Hotels or with the Riverside, you will go down. We have proof of what you did in Boston, and the only reason my father didn't pursue it at the time was out of deference to me. But I don't need protecting. I'm my own woman, and I can take care of myself. Now get the hell off my property, and stay off, or I swear, I'll make you sorry you ever heard the name Abigail Donavan."

Zachary stood for a moment, his mouth opening and closing like a fish out of water. I was about to say more when suddenly he jerked out of the doorway, like a puppet who'd been pulled off the stage.

"Pretty sure the lady told you to get the hell out, dickhead." Ryland held Zachary by the collar. The other man's feet dangled off the ground for a minute before Ryland dropped him. "I'd like nothing more than to beat the shit out of you for what you did to her, but Abby there just did a better job ripping you open than I ever could with my fists. But I'll have no issue with kicking your ass to the edge of the property if you don't move it now."

Zachary fixed his shirt and glared at first Ryland and then me. "If you touch me again, you'll be sorry. I'll have lawyers here on your ass faster than you can—"

Ryland took one step forward, and Zachary shrunk back. He hesitated another minute, and then with a muffled curse, he turned around and took off down the path, away from the hotel.

I collapsed against the wall, surprised to realize I was shaking. Ryland came toward me, taking the steps two at a time. Pulling me into his arms, he rubbed my back.

"He didn't . . . try anything, did he, Abby? He didn't hurt you?"

I shook my head. "No. He just spouted off with a lot of stupid stuff." I raised my face to look up into Ryland's eyes. "He said I was like him, cold and all business. But I'm not, right? Not anymore."

"No, baby. You're anything but cold." His voice was soothing, but I knew he was being truthful, too.

I reached up to stroke his cheek. "But I might've ended up like that if it weren't for you. God, I was close. Thank you, Ryland. Thanks for making sure I didn't turn into a frigid bitch."

He choked with what might've been laughter and held

me tighter, his lips skimming over my hair.

"Any time, baby. And all the time."

chapter thirteen

Ryland

"HEY, YOU'RE SURE THE LADY boss likes Italian, right?" Linc rounded the corner out of the kitchen. "You checked and made sure she's not allergic to garlic or oregano or anything, right?"

I rolled my eyes. "Yeah, Linc. I'm sure. She loves Italian, she doesn't have any food allergies, and whatever you make is going to be fine. Why're you so nervous about this dinner, anyway? You'd think she's your girlfriend, not mine."

Linc eyed me. "Girlfriend, huh? So it's official?"

I scowled. "Whatever, dude. It's just a word. But yeah, we've been together non-stop for a while now, I sleep just about every night at her place, and . . . yeah. Girlfriend works. For now."

He raised his hands. "Don't attack me, I was just asking. For what it's worth, I approve." He turned around. "Can you set the table? I need to check the pasta."

I'd just finished folding the napkins and tucking them next to the plates when there was a knock at the door. I heard Abby's voice from downstairs. "Ryland? Linc? Can I come in?"

I smiled. I went in and out of her apartment at will now, treating it like my second home, but that was my Abby—always careful, always courteous. Always aware of not overstepping boundaries.

"Come on up, gorgeous." I met her at the top of the steps, pulled her into my arms and kissed her. "Welcome to the bachelor pad."

She laughed and handed me a small bag. "I bought Italian bread as requested." She raised her voice. "Something smells delicious!"

Linc called back. "You better believe it, sweetheart! Hope you brought your appetite."

I led her to our small sitting area. "Glass of wine, baby? I got both red and white."

"Red, please. I can get it if you like. Will Linc be insulted if I offer to help in the kitchen?"

"Yes!" The man himself responded from beyond the doorway, and Abby and I both laughed.

"Message received." She sat down. "This is actually a sweet little apartment. Emmy acted like it was a frat house before Cooper moved out."

I nodded. "She wasn't wrong. I saw it then. I think he pretty much just slept here, and it looked it. At least he didn't mind me bringing in some furniture and making it work for Linc and me."

I poured the wine at the table and carried two glasses to the sofa. Handing one to Abby, I clinked my glass to hers. "Cheers."

"*Salut*." She sipped. "Mmmm. Nice."

"Things busy today?" I sat on the arm of the chair facing her. Abby had been spending most days in the office now as everything geared up for the hotel's opening. I missed seeing her on the job site, hearing the click of her heels. But we were close to opening, and both of us had last-minute tasks.

"Crazy. We're getting a flood of calls, and since we opened up reservations, we haven't been able to keep up with them. We have a waiting list, and that's after referring people to the Hawthorne House. Cal's been coming in to help me with the final plans. I don't know what I'd do without him."

"If there's anything I can do, just tell me." I reached for her hand and lifted the knuckles to my lips. "Don't work too hard. I want you to enjoy this opening, not be flat on your back exhausted."

She smiled. "I'll do my best. I was actually thinking—"

"Dinner is served." Linc came around the corner, carrying a large bowl of pasta. A good deal of the red sauce was splashed onto his shirt, but I decided it behooved me to keep that observation to myself.

I knew my friend was a good cook, but it was a pleasure to watch Abby discover that fact. She raved over the sauce and meatballs, had two helpings of salad—he made his own dressing—and praised the entire meal.

"Linc, if you ever get tired of this guy, I'll hire you to

cook at the Riverside." She folded her napkin in her lap. "Seriously, I think that's the best Italian food I've had since I left Philadelphia."

He tried to play it off, but I could tell Linc was pleased. "Yeah, who knows? Maybe someday we'll both get tired of living out of a suitcase and settle down." He nudged me. "But not yet, right, brother? Not when the jobs keep rolling in." He smiled at Abby. "Did he tell you about this sweet gig in St. Louis next month?"

Shit. Of course I hadn't mentioned St. Louis to Abby, because I hadn't made up my mind about it yet. Sure, I'd told Linc to accept it conditionally. I'd promised to fly up there and check it out after the Riverside opened. But that didn't mean I was committed to working it.

But as his words sank into her mind, I watched the expression on Abby's face morph from relaxed happiness to something that was akin to panic. I hadn't seen her look that way since the first night I'd tried to kiss her.

"No. No, Ryland didn't mention a job in St. Louis." She didn't look my way; instead, she focused on Linc. "Why don't you tell me about it, Lincoln?"

For all the years my best friend had been married, and for all his knowledge of the female sex, he was oblivious. I wanted to kick him under the table, but I couldn't reach him around Abby's legs. "Well, it's sweet because it's all inside work. Usually, we get to this time of year and we don't have any real jobs, since construction slows down in the cold months. But this place already has the exterior finished, so we'd just have to do the interior. A lot of wood work, moldings, fixtures, and that kind of stuff. And it pays a pretty penny, too."

"Well, that's . . . that's just wonderful, Linc. You must be excited." Even if I couldn't see her face, I would've known Abby was upset by the way she was speaking—that neutral tone, her words clipped and precise. She finally turned to look at me, and I saw the devastation in her eyes. "Have you ever been to St. Louis before, Ryland? I've been once. We looked at a hotel there. Ended up not doing it, but we did spend some time there, on and off. I think I was . . . oh, maybe fourteen or so."

"Abby, I didn't—"

"Linc, can I help you clean up? That's my rule, you know. If someone makes me a meal, I like to handle washing dishes."

Linc had finally clued into the fact that he'd said something wrong. "Uhh, no, thanks, Abby. I'm really particular about it, and I don't have anything else to do tonight. I was planning to call my kids and talk to them while I washed up, so I'd rather be alone."

"Of course." She pushed back her chair and stood up, laying her carefully folded napkin alongside the plate. "Linc, thanks very much for a wonderful meal and a lovely evening." She spared me a passing glance. "Ryland, if you don't mind, I think I'm just going to go home now. I have a terrible headache, and I'd like to lie down. Alone."

Without waiting for me to respond, Abby turned around, grabbed her purse and flew down the steps. She was out the door before I could even get to my feet.

"Dammit, Linc!" I pounded on the table, and the silverware rattled. "What the hell? Why would you say that?"

He'd dropped his head into hands. "I know. I'm so sorry, Ry. It never occurred to me—well, I thought you'd told her. You don't keep secrets."

"It wasn't a secret. I haven't made up my mind how I'm going to handle it. If I even want to take that job. I figured I'd cross that bridge after the hotel opened."

"I didn't know." Linc just kept shaking his head. "God, I'm sorry. I was just excited about the job, and I was making conversation. I didn't stop to think."

I blew out a sigh. "Not your fault. Not completely. I'm going after her, see if she'll talk to me."

When I made to the gravel lot that separated the house from the workshop, I was surprised to see Abby's car still there. And then I spotted her in the driver's seat, her head bent and her shoulders shaking.

I opened the door and knelt beside her. "Abby, baby. Don't cry. This isn't what you're thinking. It's not—"

"It's not what, Ryland? It's not you taking off, moving on? It's not the next job? The next town? The next project? It's not you leaving me?" Her voice rose on a sob that broke my heart.

"No, I haven't taken the job yet, Abby. It was an offer. I haven't decided anything."

"Linc seemed to think it was pretty much a done deal." She reached to pull the door closed. "Get away, Ryland. I want to go home. I want to be alone."

"Abby, let me come with you. We'll talk."

"I don't want to talk to you." She flashed tear-filled eyes up at me. "I'm angry at you. I'm angry at *me*. I knew better—God, when will I learn? Everyone leaves. No one

212

stays." She jerked the door handle, but it caught on my leg. "It all comes down to that, right? I was fun while you were in town, but that's it. I should've known I'm not worth staying around for."

She pulled the door again, and this time it slammed. I jumped out of the way just in time to avoid being hit by its corner. Abby started up the car, threw it into reverse and blew out of the lot, a spray of gravel in her wake.

"Sounds like you had a rough evening."

I turned to see Cooper standing in the doorway of his workshop. "You could say that. Abby misunderstood—Linc told her about a job we were offered. She thought I meant to take it, to leave the Cove. She's, uh, a little upset."

Cooper laughed. "Sorry, Ryland, but I think that's like saying the Titanic had a little leak. You got a problem, man."

I swallowed. "We didn't have any commitment. I mean, I never said I was staying in town." It sounded lame, even to my ears, and Cooper shook his head.

"Ryland, did you sleep with her? Did you act like you cared for her? And keep in mind I've been around the two of you together. I already know the answer to the second question."

I blew out a long breath. "Yeah, I slept with her. And I do care for her. I've never felt for any other woman what I feel for Abby."

"Then there's your commitment. You know her situation. You know she's not leaving town. She's a Cove girl now, and that hotel's her baby. If you knew you wanted to move on, that you planned to do it, and you weren't upfront with her—and I mean specifically upfront with her, before you two got together at all—then you're not the man I took you to be." He folded his arms over his chest and stared me down.

"I hadn't thought about it. I didn't want to think about it." I kicked some of the tiny stones on the ground. "But she never asked me to stay either, Cooper. She knows my life, and Abby never said, 'Stay with me. I need you.'"

He nodded. "Then that's something she needs to deal with. But we're talking about you now. What're going to do?"

I shrugged. "I don't know."

"Really? You don't know. You love that woman, Ryland. Get your ass over to her apartment, get down on your sorry knees, and grovel your heart out. Tell her what she needs to hear, and beg her to forgive you for being an ass." He paused. "Take it from one who knows. I was almost too stupid to keep the woman I loved. I almost let her get away. Every day of my life now, I'm grateful that I got wise before it was too late."

I thought about Abby, the hurt on her face, the words she'd said. *Everybody leaves me. I'm not worth staying around for.*

I turned for my truck.

"Where're you going?" Cooper called as I opened the door.

"To not be stupid before it's too late."

Just before I slammed the door, I heard him chuckle.

214

Abby

I drove back to my apartment almost blind with tears and pushed through the Saturday night crowd to get upstairs. I heard Emmy calling after me, but I ignored her, ran up the steps and slammed the door before I fell onto my sofa and let the sobs overtake me.

I loved Ryland. Of course I did. I'd known it for weeks now, if not months, but I didn't rush into anything because we had time. Or so I'd thought. But apparently all the time I'd thought we were building a foundation we could live on for the rest of our lives together, he was planning to leave town.

He'd never told me otherwise. I'd been a fool not to see that, not to realize that he'd made no promises. When we were planning out my suite at the hotel, he'd never mentioned living there with me. When I'd talked about the future, he'd never committed to anything beyond the day we opened the Riverside. I was stupid, blind. An idiot.

Pounding at the door jolted me to awareness. "Abby, open the door. We need to talk."

"Go away, Ryland. I'm done talking. I want to be alone." I curled into myself, willing him to leave me be.

"Abby, I'm not going away. Not tonight. Maybe not ever. Not without you. Please, baby, open the door and talk to me."

I shook my head, even though he couldn't see me. "Stop making promises you don't want to keep, Ryland. Just go. Go to St. Louis, go to Texas, go to. . .go to hell for all I care."

"Abby, I want to make promises to you. I want us to make promises to each other." He was quiet a minute. "Remember that night after our first date, when we sat in the truck, and I said I didn't want anything but you? I was wrong."

I frowned. Where was he going with this?

"Abby, I want you. But I want more. I want your future. I want your present. I want your nights and your mornings, and your afternoons. I want your weekends and your holidays. I want your laughter and your tears and your mad and your silly. I want your crappy taste in music and your Chinese food in bed and the way you call me Mr. Kent when you're about to—"

I jumped to my feet and opened the door. The music downstairs was loud, sure, but no way did I want what Ryland had been about to say to be broadcast to anyone who might be standing at the bottom of the steps.

"Yeah, I thought that would get you." He advanced into the apartment, his eyes never leaving mine, and kept walking toward me. I backed up until my heels hit my bedroom door.

"This seems familiar." He smiled down at me, wiped a tear away from my cheek and kissed my forehead. "Abby, I meant everything I said. I want all that. I want to live here in Cove with you. I don't know how we're going to make that work, with your job and mine, but that's what we're going to do. We're going to make a life together. I love you, Abby Donavan, and I never want to say good-bye to you."

Something tight and hard inside me broke, flooding my heart with more hope and joy than I'd thought possible. "I wanted you to stay. I never said it, and I should've, but I want you to stay. I know there're places you still want to see, and I know you love your work. I don't want you to resent me for keeping you here. I don't know how we'll make it work, but I want to have a life with you, Ryland. I love you. I never want to stop being in love with you."

He took my face in both of his hands. "The world is full of places and people, Abby. We'll see them together. We'll work it out. We'll make it work, our way. But you will be my one true home, forever. Always remember, no matter what might happen, I love you more." He covered my lips with his, sealing his words with a kiss that promised a lifetime of tomorrows.

the end

epilogue

I T WAS A PERFECT DAY for a party.

The sun was warm, but not hot. A cool breeze floated over the vast green lawns, rustling the palm fronds as the wind chimes on the porch rang. The sound of the river lapping gently at its banks might have drifted over the throngs of people, had the crowd not been so talkative.

But they were, and quite a crowd it was. People had come from all over to celebrate what they called a Grand Opening.

Of course, she knew it was really a rebirth.

Others had tried to make this happen, had tried to bring her back to life, but until this year, no one had succeeded. At first, she hadn't trusted them, the two who had walked her halls, at first separately and then together, speaking aloud as they vowed to repair and restore. She'd been skeptical, defensive.

But then she'd watched them work, and she watched the progress. She'd watched with burgeoning affection as love had taken root and grown between Him and Her. When the woman had run away that first time, she'd encouraged him. *Wait. She'll return.* And of course she had.

For weeks now, she'd watched them walk her grounds and throughout her buildings, holding hands, talking about the past—her past—and their future. They'd furnished the small suite where they'd begin their lives together. She'd smiled the first night they'd spent there, sighed a little at the passion the two shared.

Love belonged here.

And now there would be more. There would be guests and families and lovers and children and friends—old friends and new ones. Long-lasting love and love found anew. First love and second love and love for the ages.

She sighed, and on the front porch, near the chimes, the woman stopped talking. She sniffed the air, scenting the lilacs, and she looked around, rubbing her hands over her skin as though chilled. The man slid his arms beneath hers, glancing around as well. A smile flitted over his face, and he spoke two low words.

You're welcome.

Fitting words for such an occasion, and she smiled, knowing he felt her gratitude and appreciation. With hope brimming in her heart, she looked toward the setting sun and the promise of her new beginning.

playlist

The songs for this book were mostly suggested via the hours I've spent on the roads of America this summer. I owe a tremendous debt to Sirius XM Satellite radio, particularly to The Bridge and Love Songs, which brought back wonderful memories from my childhood years, traveling across the country. Ryland may despair of improving Abby's musical taste, but I love her just the way she is.

Goodbye To Love The Carpenters
Ready to Take A Chance Again Barry Manilow
Anticipation Carly Simon
Let Me Be There Olivia Newton-John
Close To You The Carpenters
You and Me Against the World Helen Reddy
Song Sung Blue Neil Diamond
We've Only Just Begun The Carpenters
In My Life The Beatles

acknowledgements

The summer of 2015 has been a whirlwind for me. I'm not sure I ever stopped moving, and it always felt as though I were two or three steps behind where I was supposed to be.

However, if it weren't for all these wonderful people, I would've been seriously in trouble.

My fabulous book prep team always shows an extraordinary amount of patience. Kelly Baker is my proofreader extraordinaire and doomed to remain that for time eternal. Stacey Blake of Champagne Formats takes those words and makes them into a book, all pretty and spaced just right! Stephanie Nelson of Once Upon A Time Covers did all the dreamy covers for this summer's Crystal Cove Romances. I just adore them.

Marla Wenger jumped into the fray to help with proofing for this book, too. I am so grateful and excited for her new venture as a proofer!

This summer, my partner in crime Mandie Stevens and I took a leap into an entirely new world: book event planning. We took over and ran Indie BookFest, and while at times I wondered about our joint sanity, in the end it was one of the most satisfying and fun experiences of my life. So big love to Mandie, Jen Rattie and Stacey Blake, as well as to our incredible volunteers: Maria Clark, Melanie Marsh, Tammy Richardson and Kimberly Cheeseman. Shall we do it all again . . . next year?

Thanks, too, to Maria for all her help with my author

life, to my very organized daughter Haley who has taken on the task of personal assistant and to Jen Rattie and Andrea Coventry, who are jumping in for promotions. You all make my life so much more possible!

Big love to my Temptresses, who are wicked funny, sweetly supportive and full of excellent ideas.

And always love to Clint and the kiddos, who tolerate Mommy's wacky lifestyle and help without complaining. I love you all madly.

The Crystal Cove Books
begin with

THE POSSE

See how Jude and Logan found their way to love.

Being a widow at the age of forty-four was never in Jude Hawthorne's plans. After her husband's death, she's left with her family's beach restaurant and two nearly-grown children. The last thing she's looking for is another chance at love.

However, if her husband's best friends, the Posse, have anything to say about it, love is just what she's going to get. The Posse is determined to take care of Jude, and when they decide the best way to do that is for one of them to sweep her off her feet, three begin to vie for her affections. But only one can reach her heart.

In a story of friendship, loss and second chances,

Jude will learn her life is far from being over.

about the author

Photo by Heather Batchelder

Tawdra Kandle writes romance, in just about all its forms. She loves unlikely pairings, strong women, sexy guys, hot love scenes and just enough conflict to make it interesting. Her books run from YA paranormal romance through NA paranormal and contemporary romance to adult contemporary and paramystery romance. She lives in central Florida with a husband, kids, sweet pup and too many cats. And yeah, she rocks purple hair.

Follow Tawdra on Facebook, Twitter, Instagram, Pinterest and sign up for her newsletter so you never miss a trick.

Other Books by the Author

The King Series
Fearless
Breathless
Restless
Endless

Crystal Cove Books
The Posse
The Plan
The Path

The Perfect Dish Series
Best Served Cold
Just Desserts
I Choose You

The One Trilogy
The Last One
The First One
The Only One

The Seredipity Duet
Undeniable
Unquenchable

Recipe for Death Series
Death Fricassee

Printed in the USA
CPSIA information can be obtained
at www.ICGtesting.com
JSHW031712140824
68134JS00038B/3652